Praise for RITA Award-nominated author Jane Graves

"Graves is a solid storyteller with a confident, convincing voice."
   —*Publishers Weekly*

"Jane Graves is an author whose touch is magic when it comes to creating characters that the reader can identify with, characters that stay with you long after the book is finished."
   —*Halifax Chronicle Herald*

"For every mass-market author who made the leap to hardcover, a new talent rose to take her place: Jane Graves wowed readers with her wacky debut, *I Got You, Babe*."
   —*Publishers Weekly*, "The Year in Books 2001"

"This rollicking romantic comedy explodes off the starting block...Graves's ready wit and charismatic characters are an abundant source of comic relief. Readers looking for a strong hero and a feisty heroine who face off against each other will enjoy this fast-paced tale."
   —*Publishers Weekly* on *I Got You, Babe*

"There's no question that she knows how to create suspense; she's the master of the cliffhanger chapter ending. What sets this novel apart from its peers, however, is not the suspense but the characters and their witty, warm-hearted interactions." "
   —*Publishers Weekly* on *Flirting with Disaster*

Jane Graves

Growing up, Jane Graves dreamed of becoming a veterinarian, but her high school counselor told her it was "a difficult field for a woman," so she should pick another career—perhaps something as a writer, since she had shown some talent in that area. Since her assertiveness didn't come until later in life, Jane did as she was told and went to the University of Oklahoma, where she earned a B.A. in journalism in the professional writing program.

Now the author of fourteen novels, Jane is a five-time finalist for Romance Writers of America's RITA® Award, the industry's highest honor, and is the recipient of two National Readers' Choice Awards, a Booksellers' Best Award and the Golden Quill.

Jane lives in Texas with her husband of twenty-four years, a daughter pursuing her master's degree, and a beautiful but goofy cat. She loves the writing life, so she's glad her high school counselor pushed her into the right career, even if it was for all the wrong reasons.

You can visit Jane's Web site at www.janegraves.com, or write to her at jane@janegraves.com. She'd love to hear from you!

MOOD SWING

Jane Graves

MOOD SWING

copyright © 2006 by Jane Graves

isbn-13: 9780373881017

isbn-10:   0373881010

This edition published by arrangement with Harlequin Books S.A.

® and TM are trademarks of the publisher. Trademarks indicated with
® are registered in the United States Patent and Trademark Office, the
Canadian Trade Marks Office and in other countries.

TheNextNovel.com

 HARLEQUIN®

PRINTED IN U.S.A.

—

CHAPTER 1

The problem started calmly enough one day when Susan Roth was having lunch in the hospital cafeteria, eating fast as she always did because somehow the E.R. never seemed to have enough nurses and she needed to get back. She'd just sat down, tossed her napkin in her lap and picked up her fork, when Dennis showed up and asked if he could join her. Unfortunately, she wasn't the kind of person who had an arsenal of lies or excuses handy to avoid people she didn't want to deal with, so she was stuck.

Dennis worked at the coffeehouse, in the strip center across the street from the hospital, where Susan went every day to get her morning dose of caffeine. He was maybe thirty-five. Maybe a little mental. Definitely had a nose the size of a rain-forest banana and enough body hair to survive naked on the tundra. But he had one characteristic that made him a barista par excellence: the ability to commit to memory an endless amount of overblown terminology and use it at will. And no wonder. Any man who can speak Klingon has no trouble remembering what *venti half-caf mocha light whip* means.

Dennis proceeded to make dumb, painful conversation about things Susan wanted to hear nothing about. His mother was of no interest to her and certainly not his mother's arthritis. No, she didn't think Earth had been seeded by ancient astronauts. And no, *Revenge of the Nerds* was not the most underrated comedy of all time. Once lunch was over, Susan felt as if she'd done twenty minutes of volunteer work with the socially challenged.

Then he showed up the next day.

She told herself not to worry, that Dennis wasn't actually trying to hit on her. Guys like him rarely got up the nerve to pursue a relationship. Instead, they retreated to their mothers' basements, where they got on the Internet and found virtual girlfriends who were guaranteed never to say no. That was what she told herself, anyway.

Then came day three.

"Wow, this is really cool," Dennis said, as he chased a pair of lima beans around his plate. "It's almost like we're dating, isn't it?"

Susan froze. What the hell was he talking about?

"Uh, no," she said. "It really isn't like that at all."

"Yeah, I think it is. I mean, what is a date, anyway? A man and a woman eating together and talking? That makes this a date."

"You talk, Dennis. I listen." And only half of that statement was true.

"That's okay. I like women who are good listeners. Not very many are, you know. It's always all about *them*."

Susan couldn't fathom any woman having a willing conversation with Dennis, much less dominating it. He was one of those irritating, dysfunctional men who preyed on nice, polite, unassertive women who wouldn't tell them to bug off.

Nice, polite, unassertive women like her.

Susan left the cafeteria and headed back to the E.R. in a Dennis-induced daze. A few hours later, Evie pulled her aside and asked her exactly how serious she and Dennis were. After all, she said with a sly smile, they were dating now.

Susan's mouth fell open. "What are you *talking* about?"

"Come on, Susan. Don't be coy. Patti from labor and delivery was getting coffee this afternoon, and Dennis told her he's been having lunch with you every day. Patti told Sam, and Sam told me."

"Dennis and I are *not* dating!"

Evie wiggled her eyebrows. "He thinks you are."

"He also thinks he's been abducted by aliens. Do you believe *that*?"

"Actually, yes," Evie said. "It would explain a lot."

Susan couldn't argue with that. But she could argue

with Evie's intrusiveness. If not for the severe nurse shortage in this city, people as irritating as Evie wouldn't even be employable.

Truth be told, though, Susan really didn't know why Dennis was targeting her. He was no prize, but she'd never considered herself to be one, either. She was forty-five, and by her own admission no great beauty. She had brown hair she stuck in a ponytail most of the time, brown eyes, nondescript facial features. Cellulite was gaining a foothold in the places where stretch marks hadn't already taken over, lovely souvenirs from the childbearing experience. Since her divorce a year and a half ago, just the thought of leaping back into the dating pool made her nervous. But if she ever chose to, she prayed to God that a whole school of Dennises wasn't swimming around in it.

The next day, Susan ventured into the cafeteria a full hour later than she normally ate, only to have Dennis show up again. And when he started talking about their "relationship," a sick sensation rose in her stomach. She could feel the groundswell of unfounded adoration. The ridiculous assumptions based on nothing.

The creation of a monster.

Be nice, Susan.

Even after all these years, her mother's voice still resonated inside her head. *Nice, nice, nice,* which meant avoidance rather than confrontation, so the next day Susan steered clear of both the cafeteria and the coffeehouse.

That was when the phone calls started.

Dennis called twice the first day. Three times the next. At all hours of the day and night. He left messages every time, asking her in that whiny, plaintive voice to pick up the phone, even though it should have been clear to him that hell would freeze over first. How he'd managed to get her phone number, she didn't know. He was probably one of those dangerously geeky guys who could hack into the White House computer system and start World War III.

After a few nights of not answering Dennis's calls and then waking one rainy morning to a droning alarm and a demanding teenager, Susan's nice-girl persona was fading fast.

"I forgot," her daughter said, as she poured a bowl of Fruity Pebbles cereal. "I need to bring something for teacher appreciation day."

Susan winced. Words such as those always brought back memories of that horrific evening when Lani was seven and announced, *I need a costume for the health play by tomorrow. I'm supposed to be a box of dental floss.*

"Something like what?" Susan asked.

"Like a dessert."

"You know you can sign me up for anything we can pick up at 7-Eleven on the way to school."

"They want a Bundt cake."

"That's the one with the weird pan?"

"Uh-huh."

Susan grabbed the milk and knocked the fridge door shut with her hip. "They're getting a box of Ding Dongs."

Lani did that eye-rolling thing, the one that has driven mothers crazy since the first prehistoric kid was told to stop scribbling on the cave walls.

"I *told* you they want a Bundt cake."

Susan checked her watch, as if she expected to see that a couple of extra hours had found their way into her day. "Time's a little short, Lani. I don't think I can whip up one of those in the next five minutes."

"But it's what they *want*."

"If you'd told me about this last night—"

"I said I forgot."

"But—"

"It's what they *told* me to bring!"

Susan clunked the milk carton on the table. "It's Linda Markham, isn't it? She's the one organizing this. This has Linda Markham written all over it. A Bundt cake. Good heavens. As if the rest of us have time to bake. It's no problem for her, of course. She doesn't work. She has a cook, a housekeeper, a gardener—"

Susan stopped short. Were Lani's eyes glistening?

No. Not tears. *No, no, no.* Junior-high hormones could catapult even the most benign situation into a major crisis.

Susan held up her palm. "Okay, sweetie. Okay. We can stop at the grocery store. They might not have a Bundt cake, but we should be able to find something that'll work." *And I'll use excuse #17 for why I'm late to work.*

Lani shrugged, but the tears kept coming.

"I told you I'd get the cake," Susan said, trying to sound patient. "There's no reason to cry about it."

Lani sniffed and wiped her eyes, but still she was crying.

"I *said* we'd go to the grocery store."

"I don't care about the cake."

"Then why are you—"

"Dad's getting married."

For several seconds, Susan just stood there, not moving. Don was getting married? She hadn't had so much as a date in the past year and a half, and *Don was getting married?*

"When did he tell you that?"

"Last night when I had dinner with him and Marla."

Marla. That woman made Susan absolutely crazy. Don had a lot of nerve dating a woman who was too nice to hate.

"Why didn't you tell me last night?" *And why didn't Don tell me before he told our daughter?*

Lani just shrugged.

"Well," Susan said gently, "I guess we knew this could happen, huh?"

Another shrug.

"We really should be happy for him, you know," Susan said in her best Mother of the Year voice, even though it was all she could do not to choke on the words. "Marla's very...nice."

Lani looked up, her eyes shimmering with tears. "But this means you and Dad really aren't getting back together."

Susan would have thought by now that her incompatibility with Don would have been clear to everyone on planet Earth, in distant galaxies and into the far reaches of the universe. How, after all this time, had it gotten past the one person closest to both of them?

Actually, it hadn't. Lani knew. But, in the end, all she wanted was for Mom and Dad to occupy the same household again so everyone could at least pretend things were normal. What she didn't know was that the longer two people pretended their relationship was normal when it was anything but, the worse it became for all concerned.

A few minutes later, Susan hustled Lani into the car, and on the way to the grocery store she explained again that reconciliation was never going to happen, which made Lani even more miserable. When they arrived at school, she'd dried her tears, but chances were that her classes that day were going to be a total bust. Lemon pound cake in hand, she started to scoot out of the car, only to turn back with a quizzical look.

"And who's that guy who keeps calling in the middle of the night, anyway?"

That's it, Susan thought. *I have to do something about Dennis.*

But once she got to the hospital, she'd lost track of that directive, with room in her mind for only one thought: *Don's getting married. And I'm not.*

I don't care, she told herself later that morning as she was extracting a peanut from a toddler's nose. After all, it wasn't as if she wasn't prepared for it—Don and Marla had been seeing each other for over a year. And she really did like Marla, enough that Susan had considered warning her that if she was going to marry Don, she'd better like her men to be mindlessly inconsiderate and grossly insensitive. But love was blind. There was someone for everyone and maybe true love had won out. She wished both of them well.

Deep breath. *Ah. There.*

Susan felt so rational and adultlike that she could almost chalk up the sickening twinge in her stomach to indigestion rather than envy. It was Don's life, after all, and she couldn't expect him to be a monk for the rest of it. She had just hoped he'd continue to be a monk until she found a way to stop being a nun.

Around noon, Susan couldn't face another of the vending-machine lunches she'd had for the past few days, so she ventured into the cafeteria. She waited until nearly one o'clock, but Dennis still showed up to make her bad day worse. Now she knew for sure that he had to be getting intelligence on her day-to-day movements from a source in the hospital. And she was pretty sure that source's name was Evie.

As Dennis started talking, Susan knew she should call a halt to all of this, but she'd dealt with enough crap that day already and the last thing she wanted was to deal with any more. So once again she tried to tune him out, turning her attention instead to the piece of gravy-covered cardboard on her plate. But as she was choking down the last bite, as impossible as it seemed, his loony rhetoric took a quantum leap.

"So I was thinking that maybe on Saturday night you could come over to Mom's house for dinner. How does that sound? She's a pretty good cook, you know."

Susan stopped short. "What did you say?"

"Mom told me to invite you to dinner."

She looked at him incredulously. "I don't even *know* your mother."

"That's the point. She always wants to meet the girls I date."

Susan gripped her fork until her fingers turned white. "Dennis. *We're not dating.*"

"Sure we are. We have lunch together all the time. Evie says a relationship is all about togetherness."

Evie. Change one letter and she became *Evil*. Why had Susan never noticed that before?

"I'm busy on Saturday," she said.

"Then Friday."

"I'm busy then, too."

"Then pick a day. As long as it's not Sunday. That's Mom's bingo night."

Susan couldn't take this anymore. "I have to go."

She rose and headed for the conveyor belt to dump her tray. Sure enough, Dennis got up to follow her, still yammering away, and all she could think about was how her ex-husband was getting married to a decent woman when the best Susan could do was the quintessential geek with bad hair, bad posture and bad breath, a man she was going to have to break up with even though they'd never dated in the first place.

Suddenly, all kinds of emotions swirled around inside her. Irritation. Apprehension. Resentment. Desperation. Regret over the past. Hopelessness for the future. A plan was forming in her mind to break into a Hershey's chocolate factory at two in the morning and eat herself senseless, after which she would crawl into a corner, curl up in a fetal position and cry. At that moment, she was a psychologist's Rolodex all crammed into one person, and that one person was ready to blow.

"So how about seven o'clock on Thursday?" Dennis said. "Any later and Mom's arthritis starts to—"

"Don't talk to me anymore."

"But—"

"I said shut up."

"But I need to be able to tell her—"

Susan slammed her tray down on the conveyor belt and spun around, skewering him with a furious glare. "Listen to me! I don't want to go *anywhere* with you!"

When his eyes got all wide with surprise, Susan was sure she'd scored a direct hit. Then his face morphed into a goofy grin. "Yeah, Evie told me you always play hard to get. She said you like men who won't take no for an answer."

Evie was a dead woman.

He inched closer. "She also said you like a man who talks dirty."

Susan had barely registered shock over that statement when Dennis, in the most graphic language imaginable, proceeded to tell her his fantasy about the nurse in the black hip boots and the naughty barista.

In a flurry of astonishment and disgust, Susan shoved him against a nearby wall, her hand at his throat. His eyes bugged open with surprise.

"Listen to me," she growled. "I'm not your girlfriend. I don't even like you. I've had it with you calling me at four in the morning. And the last thing I want to hear about are your sick fantasies!"

He tried to say something, but she tightened her hand on his throat, and he gagged and gasped instead.

"How would you like me to tell Mom what a deviant her son is? Huh? How would that be? Maybe I'll call her at 4:00 a.m. and let her know all about it!"

"No! You can't—"

"The hell I can't. And if you so much as breathe another word like that to me again, I'm ripping off your balls and tossing them into that big old vat of soup in the kitchen, and I don't give a damn what the health department says about it. Got that?"

Dennis's eyes grew wide and horrified. "Are you *crazy?*"

"Yeah, Dennis. *I'm* crazy."

"This is assault!"

"Assault? *Assault?* What you've been doing to me is assault! I never asked you to hang around, to call me at four in the morning, to *be there* every time I turn around!"

"I'm calling the cops!"

"Oh, bite me, you little twit!"

Ah, the words felt *good*, as if they'd been bottled up inside her for years, rattling the cage door, screaming to get out. When she finally let Dennis go, he stumbled out of the cafeteria with his forehead crinkled in Wookiee-like rage, and she couldn't have cared less. She felt as if she'd just conquered the world. No other jerk would ever pull this crap on her again. She'd scored one for geek-oppressed women everywhere. Until Mr. Right came along, she was through dealing with Mr. Wrong. And she felt that way right up to the time the cops showed up in the E.R. and arrested her for assault.

If only she'd pulled Dennis into a supply closet before going postal on him, there wouldn't have been any witnesses. He said/she said testimony never got a person convicted. But at noon in that cafeteria sat approximately fifty witnesses who didn't know the whole story, but they were quite willing to spill the part they did.

But no matter what all those witnesses said, Susan hadn't actually threatened to kill Dennis. She'd merely threatened to emasculate him and toss his balls into Baptist Memorial Hospital cafeteria's soup of the day. Unfortunately, Judge Henry Till of the fourth district court of Dallas County hadn't seen it her way. Leave it to a male judge to associate the loss of a guy's manhood with death.

Of course, her handprint on Dennis's throat hadn't helped matters, either.

After a plea bargain—*plea bargain*, as if she were a real criminal—she emerged from the experience with an attorney bill that was going to keep her in the red for the next year, along with a request for her presence at an eight-week, court-ordered anger management class. All because a certain banana-nosed freak couldn't keep his sick fantasies to himself.

Her coworkers were astonished. Lani was horrified. And Don was flabbergasted that his meek little ex-wife would go off on anyone. Apparently he had no idea what a time bomb he'd been dealing with for sixteen years.

So now, in the midst of having to deal with a demanding job, a nonexistent social life, an ex-husband tying the knot and a daughter crying over it, she was stuck in a class designed to teach her how to control her anger just when she was getting the hang of expressing it.

Yeah, life was definitely looking up.

CHAPTER 2

It was five after seven when Susan trotted up the front steps of Andrews Hall, one of the stark concrete buildings that comprised the campus of Henderson Community College. She guessed the court had struck a deal with the college to use its classrooms, which made her wonder if the other students in the building knew they were sharing facilities with hardened criminals who could go nuts and take hostages at any moment.

Once inside, she hurried down the hall to room 124, rounding the doorway to find a tiny classroom, where four of the desks had been arranged in a circle. Two women and a man were already seated. Given the briefcase beside the man and the admonishing frown he gave Susan when she entered the room, he was clearly the instructor. An endomorphic little person, he wore tattered slacks that had lost their crease years ago, a plain white dress shirt with cuffs rolled to his elbows and a pair of wire-rimmed glasses. And on his head was a tuft of hair so flaming red it would stop traffic on the tarmac at Dallas Fort Worth International.

She scurried into a seat and slung her purse over the back of it. "Sorry I'm late. I had an emergency at the hospital—"

"Seven sharp from now on. We have a lot of ground to cover."

No problem. Next time she'd just walk out at a quarter to seven and leave the acute arterial bleeding for the next shift.

"This is our class, ladies," he said. "I'm thrilled there are so few of you. Some groups are so large we have to move to another classroom, which, of course, is indicative of the societal trend toward the manifestation of anger in unhealthy and aggressive ways."

Of course.

"I'm Dr. Hugh Danforth. I have a Ph.D. in behavioral psychology. It's my job to ensure that when our eight weekly sessions are up, you'll have the tools you need to face stressful situations in a constructive manner and perhaps—" he stopped short, fanning all of them with a supercilious stare "—keep the amount of time you spend in a court of law to an absolute minimum."

Susan felt her eyes crossing. She was in for eight weeks of this? Danforth was clearly one of those guys who stroked his chin a lot and looked pensive, as if his brain was constantly at work on some esoteric Theory of Great Importance even as he was forced to muck around with individuals who didn't share his stunning intellect.

Danforth consulted his notebook. "Which one of you is Tonya Rutherford?"

The woman to Susan's right raised her hand, her metallic gold nails glinting in the fluorescent light. She had short, spiky hair in an unnatural shade of red-orange that was probably very fashionable, but it looked to Susan as if she'd dyed her hair with Mercurochrome. Her knit top and denim skirt showed way too much cleavage and way too much leg for a woman her age, which had to be close to forty. Then again, if Susan had been blessed with that woman's generous C cup, instead of her own paltry A, and if her legs weren't crawling with spider veins, maybe she'd consider baring a little more skin, too.

"What do you do for a living, Ms. Rutherford?"

"I own a hair salon."

"Please share with the class why you're here."

"Uh…a judge sent me here?" Tonya replied.

"What was the nature of your offense?"

"Oh, that. My husband had me arrested for assaulting him."

Okay, now, Susan thought. *Maybe this class will be interesting after all.*

"Specifically, Ms. Rutherford. What was the situation that culminated in your arrest?"

"Hmm. Let's see…oh, yeah. I found out my husband cheated on me. I sent a few pieces of stoneware across the room in the general vicinity of his head. He called the cops and pressed charges. I ended up with a bastard of a judge who loves creative sentencing, so here I am."

"I'd like to remind you, Ms. Rutherford, that had you not lost your temper and taken the unfortunate action you did, a judge wouldn't have had the opportunity to exercise creative sentencing."

The edge of Tonya's mouth lifted in a *screw you* smirk. "Well, then," she said, with extra emphasis on her healthy Texas twang, "I certainly apologize for my inappropriate observations about the inappropriate action the judge took as a result of my inappropriate anger."

Somewhere in the middle of all that there was an inappropriate comment, but Danforth let it go. Either that or he wouldn't recognize sarcasm if it bit him on the nose.

"Monica Saltzman?"

The woman to Susan's left came to attention. Actually, she already was at attention, one of those women born with excellent posture who didn't know the meaning of the word *slouch*. Dressed in a silk blouse and tweed pants with coordinating handbag and shoes, she was the picture of polished professionalism. As a nurse, Susan was good at spotting women who'd had work done, and this woman hadn't. Still, at least at first glance, she could pass for thirty-five, even though early forties was more likely.

Susan, on the other hand, knew she looked every day of her forty-five years. Sitting there now between Miss Brass and Miss Class, wearing puke green scrubs and sensible sneakers, she felt like a frumpy nobody.

"What is your occupation?" Danforth asked.

Monica tucked a strand of her sleek, dark hair behind her ear with one perfectly polished nail and raised her chin, pausing a moment before speaking, as if she were one of those women who expected everyone to stop whatever they were doing and hang on her every word.

"I'm an executive assistant," Monica said, then paused. "Was."

"The nature of your offense?"

"My boss shared some rather disconcerting news with me," she said. "I was quite justifiably angry, and I let him know how I felt about it."

"In what manner did you express those feelings?" Danforth asked.

She stared at him evenly. "His Hummer may never be the same again."

"Oh, yeah?" Tonya said, leaning in, her eyes wide with anticipation. "What exactly did you do to it?"

Monica's chin rose another notch. "I put a flower-pot through the windshield."

"That's it?" Tonya slumped with disappointment. "So why did you get arrested for assault when it wasn't a human being you beat up? I mean, it's a crime to destroy personal property, but—"

"He was in the driver's seat at the time."

Tonya sat back, her grin returning. "Oh. Well. Now you're talking."

"And what was the disconcerting news that sent you on this rampage?" Danforth asked.

Susan drew back. Rampage? As if she were Godzilla ravaging Tokyo?

"I don't see the need to go into the details," Monica said.

"Part of the therapy is recognizing what triggers your anger, and unless I know your threshold—"

"Fine," Monica said. "If you must know, he promised me a job, then turned around and gave it to somebody else. So you see, what I did was perfectly understandable."

"No, Ms. Saltzman. What you did was criminal."

Monica opened her mouth as if to reply, then closed it again, a slightly more refined version of Tonya's *screw you* smirk edging across her face.

Danforth scribbled something in his notebook, then turned his gaze to Susan. "You must be Susan Roth. Your occupation?"

"I'm an E.R. nurse."

"Please share with the class the act of violence that caused you to be here today."

Good Lord. This was beginning to feel like third grade show-and-tell and the Jerry Springer show all rolled into one.

Susan told her story, emphasizing just how much of

an intrusive little geek Dennis was before she revealed what led to her handprint on his throat. She thought she'd been pretty comprehensive, only to have Danforth bug her for more details.

"I just threatened him," Susan said. "That's all."

"Verbal threats frequently precipitate physical violence. Once spoken into being, they have a way of manifesting themselves into reality. It's the continuum of violence. What did you threaten to do?"

Susan looked at the other women, who were suddenly paying close attention, then back to Danforth.

"If you must know, I threatened to rip off his balls and toss them into the hospital cafeteria's soup of the day."

Danforth's already pale complexion turned as white as Elmer's glue. Gradually he moved behind the lectern, as if he felt the need to have something substantial between Susan and his privates.

"I see," he said. "We'll…uh…be doing some cognitive restructuring exercises aimed at preventing that kind of behavior."

Tonya turned to Danforth. "So you actually think if she doesn't have all her cognitive whatever restructured, someday she's actually going to tear the guy's balls off?"

Danforth cleared his throat. "I'm merely saying that if one can control one's verbiage, one can frequently control one's behavior."

"It wasn't as bad as it sounds," Susan said. "Really. I swear it wasn't."

"So you have no remorse for the act," Danforth said. "You're merely sorry you were arrested for it?"

"Well, no, I didn't mean—"

"We'll be working on that."

Susan glanced at Monica, then Tonya. They matched her subtle eye roll with ones of their own, bringing them into conspiracy together with a single common thought: *No matter what this idiot says, sometimes when people get out of line, you just gotta let 'em have it.*

Danforth launched into a lecture about the difference between assertion and aggression, and, for the next hour and a half, Tonya interrupted him every few minutes to ask him to define the terms he was using, such as *cognitive distortion* and *neuroanatomy of anger*. Susan got the feeling Tonya didn't give a damn about the definitions, but she sure liked messing with Danforth. Monica spent most of the class wearing a distinctly bored expression as if all of this was *so* not worth her time.

Susan occupied herself by going over her mental to-do list, which she had to kick into action when she got home: check to make sure Lani had done her homework; do a load of laundry so she'd have something to wear to work tomorrow; pay the overdue electric bill; call Don and remind him about Lani's basketball game. Then take a shower, climb into bed and dream of a world where money was plentiful, conflict was scarce and she had at least a few hours a day when she wasn't somebody's mother, somebody's nurse, somebody's ex-wife, or, in Dennis's case, somebody's worst nightmare.

Finally, at ten till nine, Tonya asked Danforth if he thought there was any difference between being angry, being livid and being pissed off. He looked at her dumbly for a moment. Then he took off his glasses, rubbed the bridge of his nose and dismissed class.

Susan left the classroom and headed for the bathroom. Tonya and Monica followed. They each went into a stall, and a few minutes later they were standing at the sink.

"Could you believe that guy?" Tonya said, swiping on enough lipstick to send Maybelline stock soaring. "I've never seen such a self-important little creep in my life."

"He's definitely on my top-ten list," Monica said, touching up her makeup with the precision of a microsurgeon. The compact she held looked unfamiliar to Susan, which meant it had come from somewhere besides Walgreens.

"Cognitive restructuring," Tonya muttered. *"Please."* She held up a middle finger. "Wonder how he'd like to restructure *this?*"

Monica raised an eyebrow. "You're not a particularly subtle person, are you, Tonya?"

"As if you are? I noticed you made a pretty obvious statement with that flowerpot."

"Yes. Well."

"Not that I don't admire you for it. A boss who promises you a job and then gives it to somebody else had better expect a faceful of broken glass." Tonya leaned into the mirror to wipe a stray bit of lipstick from the corner of her mouth, which made her too-short denim skirt hike even farther up her thighs. "And the little geek you went off on deserved it, too," she said to Susan. "So what if you threatened to castrate him? You were in a hospital, weren't you? They're doing wonders these days with all kinds of reattachment surgeries."

Susan smiled. After her ex-husband, her daughter, her coworkers and a certain Dallas County judge had acted as if she were criminally insane, she liked having somebody's stamp of approval, even if that somebody was just as criminally insane as she was.

"And if your husband cheats," Susan said, "I think he should expect a few flying dishes."

"I agree," Monica said.

So they'd reached a consensus. They'd all been rail-roaded. Susan suddenly felt a weird kind of camaraderie she hadn't expected, as if it were the three of them against Dr. Pompous.

She said goodbye to the other women and left the bathroom, thinking about the hundred other ways she could productively spend this one evening a week. Then again, the women's magazines always said that a working mother needed a hobby or activity away from her family and coworkers that was uniquely her own. Courtesy of the criminal justice system of Dallas County, it looked as if Susan had found one.

CHAPTER 3

Later that night, Tonya pulled her Ford Fiesta to the curb in front of her house, half expecting to see Kendra Willis's car in the driveway getting cozy with Dale's 4 x 4, while Kendra was in the house getting cozy with Dale. But the only other car she saw was Cliff's old Buick with the bad transmission, which was undoubtedly leaking fluid all over the driveway.

The living room blinds were open. The two men sat sprawled on the sofa with their feet on the coffee table, which meant they were probably watching Monday night football, and that irritated the hell out of Tonya. Her husband was in there drinking beer and watching the game with one of his firefighter buddies, while she sat out there with her hands clenching the steering wheel and her heart tied up in knots.

Two weeks ago, after the court proceedings, she'd given him the cold shoulder—no talk, no sex, no nothing—just so he'd never forget how pissed she was. When he hadn't seemed to care about that, she'd gotten progressively more frustrated, until one day she lost it a little and gave him an ultimatum. She told him that if he didn't apologize for everything he'd done and swear he'd never look at another woman again, she was going to leave. He told her he wasn't apologizing for anything. Then he went into the kitchen, grabbed a beer and a sack of pretzels and headed for the living room, where he sat down on the sofa and flipped on a NASCAR race.

It stunned her so much that she said fine, packed some clothes, her toothbrush and her makeup and told him she'd be in the apartment over her hair salon whenever he came to his senses.

A week later, she was still there.

Go, she told herself. *Drive away. Go back to your apartment and stay there until you get that apology you've got coming.*

But deep inside she had the most horrible feeling that the week she'd already waited would turn into two weeks, then three, and then Dale would realize he didn't need her after all and she'd go to the mailbox one day and the divorce papers would be there.

Tonya lit a cigarette and took a hard drag, forcing herself to think. Finally she decided that the house was hers, too, so of course she had a right to walk in anytime she wanted to. And she looked just hot enough tonight that she was sure to get Dale's attention. He'd always told her he didn't like her wearing this particular skirt around other men because they couldn't keep their eyes off her. Maybe if she strutted through the living room, Cliff's gaze would wander a little, and then Dale's possessive streak would take over and he'd want her to come home. Men weren't like women. Sometimes you had to get right in their faces to remind them of what was important.

She took a last drag on her cigarette and ground it out in the ashtray, before popping a few Tic Tacs. After checking her makeup and putting on more lipstick, she took a deep breath and got out of the car. On the way to the door, she made up a reason why she'd dropped by just in case Dale didn't jump right up and beg her to stay. But she hoped he would, if for no other reason than that he hadn't had sex in a week.

Unless he'd gone back for another round with Kendra Willis.

Shoving that horrible thought aside, Tonya stuck her key in the lock and opened the door. Dale came to attention right away, and when their eyes met, she smiled. Just a little. And when he sat back on the sofa, his face stoic, her heart crumbled.

"Now, don't you boys get up on my account," Tonya said, with just the right amount of offhanded sarcasm, as if she really didn't give a damn about any of this. "I just came by for a few things."

She went into their bedroom, where she found the

bed neatly made. That didn't surprise her. Whenever she told other women that Dale actually did housework, they always said, *All those good looks, and he helps out, too?* It had always made her feel so good to be able to give them a superior little smile that said, *you bet he does, and he's all mine.*

But that wasn't true. He wasn't all hers. Not anymore.

She pulled back the bedspread a little and gave the pillowcases a sniff, relieved to find no evidence of Kendra's god-awful perfume. They just smelled like Dale. She leaned in closer and inhaled again.

"Tonya?"

She spun around to see Dale leaning against the door frame, his arms folded, those big, beautiful biceps bulging.

"What are you doing?" he asked.

"I told you, honey," she said, dropping the bedspread and heading for the closet. "I came to pick up a few things."

She opened the door and blindly pulled a few sweaters off hangers, then grabbed a pair of shoes.

"Those are sandals," he said. "It's forty degrees out."

"Fashion before comfort, you know?"

"Did you go to your first class tonight?"

"Of course I did. Legally speaking, I didn't have a choice, now did I?"

"Because we're not going to work this out until you learn to control your temper."

"We're not going to work this out," she said, "until you stop screwing other women."

The moment the words were out of her mouth, she wished she could yank them back. Making him mad wasn't going to help things. A little shaky, she turned to grab another sweater.

"Why are you really here?" Dale asked.

"To get some things, like I told you. Oh, yeah. And I was thinking maybe you'd want to give me that apology I've been waiting for."

"It's the other way around. You assaulted me."

"Yeah, and you cheated on *me*."

"I've denied that all I'm going to."

"And you called the police on me, too. That was really low."

"It wasn't the first time you'd thrown a few dishes around. Enough was enough."

"But calling the cops?" She rolled her eyes. "Didn't the boys down at the station house think that was a little wussy?"

"Nope."

"Why not?"

"They've all met you."

The insult hurt more than she would have imagined. "You're six-three, two-twenty! Like I could actually hurt you?"

"Size doesn't matter."

Tonya snorted. "Is that what Kendra Willis told you?"

He turned away. "Take the clothes and go."

As Dale disappeared down the hall, Tonya felt her eyes tear up. *No. Don't you dare cry.*

She sniffed a little and blinked a lot until she finally got herself under control. Then she strode out of the room with her sweaters over her arm and that stupid pair of sandals dangling from her fingers.

Damn it, damn it! How had everything gotten all turned around? She hadn't wanted to fight with him. She'd wanted to make up with him and enjoy all the perks that went along with that. She missed his big, strong body wrapped around hers at night, his warm breath against her ear, the slow, steady beating of his heart. Just the idea of him holding another woman like that was more than she could bear.

She went back into the living room, where Dale and Cliff were whooping up a storm over a Cowboys touchdown. At the sound of her footsteps, Cliff turned around. His smile evaporated, and he gave her a look that said he hoped she wasn't thinking about grabbing a few cups and saucers to use as projectiles.

Dale didn't bother to look at her at all.

Tonya left the house, resisting the urge to slam the door behind her. She got into her car and reached down to start the engine, only to have her eyes fill with tears again.

Men cheat.

She'd heard her mother say that since Tonya was old

enough to remember. With three cheating husbands, her mother probably knew what she was talking about. *The minute you give a man an inch*, she always said, *he'll take a mile*.

And her mother had never given an inch. Not one.

Tonya still remembered cowering in the hall when she was seven years old, listening to her mother screaming accusations at her father. When he left for work the next day, her mother had dumped his stuff on the front lawn and changed the locks on the doors, telling Tonya that her father was gone and to quit crying because they were better off without him.

Two stepfathers came next, and the story was the same. Through it all, Tonya grew more and more suspicious of men and their motives. At the same time she would lie awake at night and imagine a forever kind of love with a man who would want her and only her. It was nothing but a fairy tale, of course, but that didn't keep her from wanting it.

Then, when she was twenty-three, Jared had come into her life, a charming motorcycle mechanic with a line of bull a mile long. Six months into a marriage that seemed to be going along just fine, she saw his car parked at a no-tell motel on the east side of town. When she confronted him about it later, he spun some story about stopping by to see a buddy from out of town who was staying there.

Relieved, she had told the other stylists at work

what had really been going on. To her surprise, they
had laughed out loud. Tonya had shouted at them to
shut up, telling them that Jared loved her and would
never cheat on her. A week later she had dropped by
his shop unexpectedly and found him and a slutty little
blonde going at it on the ugly vinyl sofa in his office,
and she wondered how many other times it had
happened that she'd never known about. That was the
moment she had come to believe wholeheartedly that
her mother was right.

Give them an inch and they'll take a mile.

Eventually she'd had to tell the girls what had
happened and face the humiliation. They'd acted
sympathetic, but she could see that look in their
eyes. *You're such a sap. Didn't we tell you he was a
cheating fool?*

Tonya had walked away from that experience wondering if, like red hair or brown eyes, attracting
cheating men ran in families, and for the next twelve
years she believed that her dream of a forever kind of
love was well and truly gone.

Then she met Dale.

She turned and looked back at the house, at Dale
lounging on the sofa. No matter how big a fool it made
her, she still wanted him so much she could barely
breathe. She thought she'd been in love with Jared, but
she knew now that she couldn't possibly have been
because he had never made her feel the hot, breath-

less, swooping sensation that came over her every time she looked at Dale.

But now everything was a big, fat mess. Was she supposed to listen to his lame excuses the way she'd listened to Jared's? Defend him? Tell everyone that even though it looked bad, of course he'd never cheat on her?

If she did, she had the most terrible feeling that the joke was going to be on her again.

She wiped away her tears and started the car, intending to go to her apartment and stay there until hell froze over if she had to. She refused to be a silly little fool who went back to a cheating man as if she had no self-respect at all. Unless he apologized and promised never to do it again, Dale wasn't going to have a chance of getting her back.

At nine o'clock the next morning, Monica sat in the lobby of Cargill & Associates, a cramped office inside a low-rent building filled with plastic ferns, walnut-veneer furniture and dollar-store art. Behind the reception desk sat a young redhead with a ring on every finger and probably a few on her toes, sipping a cup of Starbucks. On Monica's arrival, the woman had her fill out the obligatory application. She said Mr. Cargill was tied up right now, but he'd be with her in a minute, then turned her attention back to a dog-eared copy of *Cosmopolitan*, moving her lips as she read about the seven ways to drive her boyfriend wild in bed.

Monica closed her eyes for a moment, trying to calm her churning stomach. *How in the hell had it come to this?*

Thirty-two résumés, eleven job applications, four interviews and four no-thank-yous. *That* was how.

No. She had to stop thinking about how she'd failed so far and focus instead on how she could succeed. She knew how lightweight her résumé was, so she was going to have to compensate for her lack of skills in other ways.

She unfastened another button of her blouse and spread the neck apart, calling attention to the one asset of hers that men had never been able to ignore. She turned in her chair to allow the slit of her skirt to inch open farther. Then she pulled her shoulders back, lifted her nose a notch and assumed an air of total indifference, because the only people who got jobs were those who acted as if they didn't need them, even though she needed this one badly. Once Cargill came out to the lobby and she had his attention, she'd slink into his office like a lioness and go in for the kill.

She heard a door open. "Ms. Saltzman?"

Count to three, she told herself. *Don't act too eager.*

With a studied grace that came from all her beauty pageant years, Monica slowly turned her head for her first look at her future boss. And for another count of three, she gritted her teeth and tried not to cry.

She was used to bosses who wore raw silk and Italian leather. This guy was double-knit polyester and leatherette. He was pushing sixty, with a shiny scalp showing through an embarrassing comb-over and a hefty set of jowls tumbling over his shirt collar. If the guy happened to smile, which at the moment didn't seem likely, she was sure he'd have tobacco-stained teeth.

He wore no wedding ring. No surprise there.

She took a deep, calming breath, reminding herself of her dwindling savings and the mortgage payment she wasn't going to be able to make in a few months if she didn't get a paycheck coming in soon.

She rose from her chair, gave him a dazzling smile and extended her hand. "Hello, Mr. Cargill," she purred, like the lioness she was. "It's a pleasure to meet you."

His eyes never met hers. She was used to that from men because they were usually busy checking out other parts of her body. But when he didn't bother looking at any of the rest of her, either, she felt a shot of apprehension.

He gave her hand a cursory shake. "This way."

She followed him into his office, where he plopped down in his pseudo-leather executive chair.

"Catch the door," he said.

Strike one: he was ugly. Strike two: he had no manners. God only knew what strike three was going to be. Just the thought of unleashing her feminine charm on this man was making her a little queasy.

She closed the door and took a seat. He slouched

in his chair as he looked at the application she'd filled out, frowning the whole time. "It says here your most recent experience was as an executive assistant to a bank vice president."

"That's right."

"You worked for him for five years."

"Yes."

His frown deepened. "I'm not seeing much computer experience. What programs do you know?"

"Well, Word, of course. And Excel. And maybe a little bit of PowerPoint."

"Those are pretty much the baseline. What else do you have?"

Not a blessed thing. Her job at First Republic Bank had been to keep Jerry Womack's calendar, make travel arrangements, answer his calls, chat up any clients who came by for meetings, order lunch and look like a million dollars.

In the past five years, while she'd been working her way toward the forty-fourth-floor executive suite where the espresso machine was the most complicated thing she'd have to run, technology had taken a quantum leap. Unfortunately, she hadn't leaped along with it.

"What about office machines?" Cargill said. "Typing?"

She could type. Just not very well. As far as office machines, a simple phone system, a fax machine and a copier were about the only things she was sure she could handle.

If he persisted in this useless line of questioning, they were going to get nowhere.

"Let's cut right to the chase here, Mr. Cargill." She leaned in and folded her arms on his desk, slowing her words and letting her voice drop to a deeper register. "You and I both know that you can hire just about anyone to perform all those technical tasks. But that's not what makes an executive assistant so valuable, is it? In the end, there's only one qualification that's even worth talking about." She fixed her gaze tightly on his, giving him a smoldering look that had been known to bring men to their knees. "What you need, Mr. Cargill, is an assistant who can anticipate your every need—" dramatic pause "—and fill it."

She nearly choked on the words, even though they were something she could easily take back later. *You thought I meant what?* Her words appeared to have the desired effect. He sat up slightly, his bland brown eyes widening with interest. His gaze roved over her face, dropped slowly to her breasts, hovered there for a moment or two, then rose again—every flick of his eyelashes so blatantly assessing that she knew she had him on the hook.

Five seconds passed. Then ten. And no matter how unsightly he was, she forced herself not to look away.

"I'm sorry," he said, "but I don't think you're qualified for the job."

Monica felt a jolt of shock, followed by a deluge of

humiliation. He tossed her application onto his desk, pushed away from it and stood up.

Oh, God. He was brushing her off. How could this be happening?

"But…but I'm a very fast learner," she said, "if only you'll give me a chance."

"I don't think so."

"I know I'm a little shy on technical knowledge, but I'm perfectly willing to—"

"Thank you, Ms. Saltzman."

Just like that, rock bottom sank even lower.

Monica rose from her chair, feeling a little shaky, but she forced herself to thank him for his time and walk away with her chin up because she had more class than this big, blind bozo could ever hope to have.

She opened the door to his office and stepped into the lobby. Another woman was waiting there now to be interviewed, a platinum blonde who looked as if she'd cut cheerleader practice short to make it on time. And suddenly a different man was standing in Cargill's fake leather shoes.

"Well, hello, there," he said with a smile, practically tripping over himself to usher the woman into his office. As he closed the door behind them, Monica stared with disbelief, feeling like a wallflower at a high school dance.

"Well, she's a shoo-in," the receptionist said.

"Why do you say that?"

"Because she's got all the qualifications he's looking for, if you know what I mean." She rolled her eyes. "You're lucky he didn't hire you."

"Why?"

She leaned over and whispered. "Because he's a dirty old man. I've got more bruises on my ass than I can count."

When she turned back to her *Cosmo*, it occurred to Monica that she used to read that magazine herself when she was younger.

About twenty years younger.

During the other job interviews she'd had recently, she'd told herself that she just wasn't pouring on enough charm to get the attention of her prospective employers in a tight job market. But now she had to face the truth: she had nothing left that even a man like Cargill would be interested in.

One of two things was going to happen here. She was going to cry, or she was going to get mad. Since getting mad had recently bought her eight weeks in an anger management course, she left the office and hurried down the hall to the ladies' room, where she grabbed a tissue from her purse just in time to keep mascara-laden tears from rolling down her cheeks.

She turned her gaze up to the mirror, leaning in to take a closer look at herself, and maybe for the first time in years, she saw herself as she really was.

Lines she swore had never been there before fanned

out from her eyes. Skin sagged slightly at her jawline. Wrinkles had crept onto her neck. She'd been coloring her hair for so long that it could be gray all over by now for all she knew. But time had marched on, in spite of all her efforts to halt it.

All her life she'd had only one thing going for her, and that was her looks. It seemed to astonish everyone that anyone so strikingly beautiful could have been raised in such a dirt-poor family. In light of that, her mother had dragged her to beauty pageants from the time she was old enough to twirl a baton. She learned how to wink at those judges long before she knew that about half of them were dirty old men who loved looking up little girls' skirts. Because she'd always been told she was all beauty and no brains, she'd goofed off in school and skipped college, doing what a lot of beautiful but brainless girls did—she set out to marry a rich man. And she'd almost accomplished that goal. Three times. But something always happened to nip her plans in the bud.

The first man had a wife he hadn't bothered to tell her about. The second one decided, after a three-year relationship, that it was time for him to come out of the closet. The third time around, when Monica actually had a ring on her finger, she told herself that for the Highland Park lifestyle, she could overlook her fiancé's drinking habit. And she did, right up to the moment he got his third DUI and a judge threw the book at him. Conjugal visits during that five-year sentence just hadn't seemed all that appealing to her.

Somehow she turned thirty-five. Then she was pushing forty. During those years, she hadn't bothered to acquire job skills beyond basic clerical ones, telling herself that marriage was just around the corner, only to realize that the pool of wealthy, available men was drying up, at least those wealthy, available men interested in her. And she was still working in the same low-paying, dead-end jobs she had been for the past fifteen years, so her financial future looked pretty bleak.

Then, one night at an uptown bar, she met Jerry Womack, a vice president at First Republic Bank. He was fifty-four and recently divorced. As he stared at her breasts, he told her his executive assistant was leaving and Monica might be just the woman he was looking for to replace her. The next day when she went to his office to talk to him, she discovered that the job came with a bigger paycheck than she'd ever seen in her life and very few responsibilities.

At least, very few responsibilities within the confines of the office.

At first, the whole situation made Monica a little sick to her stomach. Marrying rich was one thing, but putting out to keep a job was something else.

But the money. God, the *money*.

Suddenly she could afford to shop at Neiman Marcus rather than sift through the junk at outlet stores. She could buy a car that didn't end up in the shop once every three months. She could afford a condo in a decent neighborhood rather than rent an apartment next door to a guy she was pretty sure was dealing crack.

So she did it, telling herself that maybe one day she'd marry that boss she was sleeping with. A couple of times Jerry even suggested it might be a possibility. So when the bank president had retired and Jerry ascended to that position, Monica had been thrilled. Only, it wasn't Monica whom Jerry decided to bring with him to the executive suite. It was pretty, perky, *young* Nora O'Dell.

You understand, Jerry had the nerve to say. *It's just business.*

So she showed him some business in the form of a flowerpot right thought the windshield of his lemon-yellow Hummer. And right now, she was thinking about the fake potted palm in the corner of Cargill's office, wondering what kind of car he drove.

No. She had to get Cargill out of her mind. This had just been a fluke. He was simply a man who needed to rescue his own aging self-image by surrounding himself with young women. And losing out on those other four interviews had simply been a run of bad luck. That was all.

She repaired her makeup and left the bathroom, telling herself that everything was going to be fine, that a new job was just around the corner. Still, it was hard to ignore the scary little ball of nerves rolling around in her stomach, the one that was telling her that finding a job was going to be a far greater challenge than she'd ever anticipated.

CHAPTER 4

The gymnasium at Parker Heights Middle School was old, musty and smelled like dirty athletic socks, and every time Susan climbed the bleachers to sit on one of the metal benches, she actually wished she were back in the hospital, which smelled like antiseptic and sick people. The bounce of basketballs echoing off the gym walls and the squeak of shoes on the wood floors grated on her nerves the way nails against a blackboard grated on other people's. But she still showed up with a smile on her face, cheering when she was supposed to, because that was what moms did.

She sat down on a bench by herself, thinking about how she'd always felt sorry for the single and divorced moms who showed up alone to school events. They always had that look in their eyes as if they were frantically trying to remember everything they had to do. At the same time there was a droopy-shouldered weariness about them that said completion of those tasks was going to be impossible. Now she was one of them. Of course, in a world where divorces were more common than lifelong marriages, she was really just a face in the crowd.

She turned to see Lani hopping up the bleachers. "Mom, gimme a hair scrunchie."

Susan dug through her purse, eventually having to put half its contents on the bench beside her before finally locating one wound around a box of Band-Aids. Lani grabbed it and swooped her hair toward the crown of her head.

"Where's Dad?" she asked.

"I don't know."

"Did you remind him?"

"Yes, honey. I reminded him."

"Did you tell him I was starting?"

"Yes."

"Then why isn't he here?"

"I'm sure he'll be here soon."

She hoped he would be, anyway, because Lani didn't handle it well when he didn't show up. Lani didn't handle much of anything well these days. Susan's happy, perky daughter of a few years ago seemed to have vanished, replaced by an adolescent girl whose moods were so volatile that Susan never knew what she was in for from one moment to the next. In the span of an hour, she could go from crying to laughing to being angry to shutting down communication completely, and there was no way to predict which one it was going to be.

"He didn't come to my last game," Lani said.

"He had to work late."

"I'm starting tonight. What if he doesn't get here until the second half?"

Lani! We're divorced! Don't ask me these questions! Ask him!

"He told me he was coming, so I'm sure he'll be here."

Lani frowned. "Is he bringing Marla with him again?"

"I really don't know."

"I hope not. It's weird when she's here."

Susan had to agree with that.

Lani hopped back down to the gym floor to warm up with her teammates. Susan had thought when she signed those divorce papers it meant she was no longer her husband's keeper, but somehow it hadn't turned out that way. She stuck all the stuff she'd unloaded from her purse back into it again.

"Hello, Susan."

At the sound of the woman's voice, Susan turned around to see Linda Markham sitting down next to her. *Please. Not her. Not now. Not anytime.*

"I just wanted to thank you for the pound cake you sent for Teacher Appreciation Day," Linda said.

Which had been a while back, so what did she really want? "You're welcome."

"I think on the whole the teachers enjoyed it, even though it wasn't homemade."

Speaking of not homemade, you came this *close to getting a box of Ding Dongs.* "Oh, I'm so glad," Susan said. "I'm just so rushed some days that it's hard to fit everything in."

"I'm sure it is. If you'd like, I can recommend a wonderful time-management course. Why don't I e-mail you the information?"

Why don't you shove the information? "How sweet of you, Linda. I'd really appreciate that."

"And next time, just let me know if you don't have a Bundt cake pan. I have three. I'd be happy to let you borrow one."

She gave Susan an angelic little smile, but Susan was sure she could see horns sprouting from the top of her head. Linda was one of those insidious women who masked their condescending nature with just enough cutesy smiles and sweet words that you couldn't come back at them without looking like an ungrateful bitch. Susan's theory was that motherhood was the only identity Linda had, so becoming queen bee of Parker Heights Middle School was her pinnacle of success. She'd guilt-tripped all the mothers into following after her like a bunch of mind-numbed minions, but still Susan wondered... If one of them ever got up the nerve to toss a bucket of water on Linda, would the others cheer as she melted?

Then Linda put her hand on Susan's arm and dropped her voice. "Tell me, Susan. How are things since the divorce? Lani seems to be holding up well, but how are you?"

"It's been a year and a half," Susan said. "I'm good. But thank you so much for asking."

"I know how difficult it can be. Not personally, of course. But I've had acquaintances who were divorced. It's such a traumatic thing."

Then she leaned in and spoke softly. "Is it true what I hear? That Don is getting married again?"

"Yes. It's true."

"So how do you feel about that?"

How do I feel about it? As if I'm losing some kind of race I never wanted to enter in the first place. That's how I feel.

"His fiancée is a nice person," Susan said. "I'm sure they'll be very happy together."

"Oh, sweetie," Linda said, patting Susan's arm. "You're so brave."

Susan had discovered that wrapping her hand around the neck of somebody who was bugging her didn't make her feel that bad, and right now making history repeat itself was a pretty tantalizing thought.

Linda's gaze drifted to one side. "Oh, I suppose I'd better hush. There's Don."

Susan turned, relieved to see her ex coming up the stairs. As Linda scurried away, Don sat down beside Susan, one of Lani's textbooks under his arm.

"You were talking to Linda Markham?" he said.

"Yeah. Didn't you know? We're best friends."

"Right." He shook his head. "I always wondered what it would be like to be married to a woman who was that uptight. She probably keeps her vagina under lock and key."

Susan blinked with astonishment.

"What?" Don said.

"Do you know that in all the time I've known you, I've never once heard you utter the word *vagina?*"

He shrugged. "I always thought it would embarrass you."

Right. She was an E.R. nurse. She blushed at the mere mention of genitalia.

No. If anybody had been embarrassed by the word *vagina,* it had been Don. He'd been the "lights out, no talking" kind of lover who would flatline any woman's libido. But given the glow that seemed to surround Marla these days, evidently Don had gotten a whole new attitude where sex was concerned. They weren't actually living together, which relieved Susan from having to deal with Lani's feelings about *that* issue, but "not living together" didn't mean "not having sex."

Or maybe he'd finally found a woman who actually turned him on.

"Lani's math textbook," Don said, handing her the book under his arm. "She left it at my house yesterday."

Susan took the book with a sigh. "What are we going to do about her forgetting stuff?"

"I don't know. Maybe you should talk to her."

"I have talked to her, Don. About a dozen times."

"She'll grow out of it."

Yes, and in the meantime Lani would continue to get zeros on assignments she left at home. *Thanks for the insight, Don.*

Susan asked "So where's Marla?"

"Late getting off work. She'll be here soon."

Susan didn't know how she felt about Marla being so diligent about coming with Don to Lani's games. Nice Susan thought it was a good thing to do, particularly since she and Don were getting married. But Bitter Susan was getting a little tired of Marla being so sweet and kind. Damn it, just *once* couldn't she do something rotten and bitchy?

"There's something I need to talk to you about," Don said. "Marla and I are going away for the three-day weekend coming up, so I won't be able to see Lani."

"Going away? Where to?"

"San Francisco."

Susan looked at him dumbly. "You're flying to San Francisco for the weekend?"

"It's kind of a spur of the moment thing." He smiled. "We like being spontaneous."

No, you don't. Or, at least, you didn't. What happened?

Susan couldn't believe this. In sixteen years of marriage, Don had never once taken her anywhere on a plane. If they couldn't get to it within five hours by car after weeks of planning, they didn't go. It was a travel mentality that had led to some ultra-exciting trips to Sea World, the Best Western on Galveston beach and the Alamo, usually with Lani in tow. And now he was taking Marla to San Francisco, which meant a beautiful hotel, whirlwind sightseeing and romantic dinners.

All Susan had ever gotten was an ear infection at Hurricane Harbor.

"Why don't you take Lani with you?"

Don went pale. "Take Lani?"

"Why not? If Marla's going to be part of the family, it can be like a family vacation."

"Uh…yeah. But I really hadn't intended—"

"Intended what?"

"You know, we have just one room booked, and—"

"Then it'll be really cozy, won't it?"

"Uh…"

"Just say it, Don. You want to go away with Marla over the weekend, and you don't want anything messing up all that fun you'd planned on having in the bedroom."

Don looked relieved. "Then you do understand."

Lord, this man was such a dimwit sometimes. "So what about *my* bedroom activities?"

He looked at her dumbly. "What bedroom activities?"

"Exactly," Susan said. "I don't have those. Not with a fourteen-year-old in the house."

"So are you dating someone?"

"Did you hear what I said? *I have a fourteen-year-old in the house.*"

"Lani's with me every Saturday and other times if you need me to take her. Why can't you date then?"

"Because by the time Saturday rolls around, I'm too damned tired to do anything, much less get all dressed up to go out. That's why."

Susan didn't like the way she sounded, all cranky and whiny and defensive. But the truth was that as much as Don saw Lani, Susan still felt like a single parent. Don merely visited every once in a while, took her out, bought her things, then brought her back home, where Susan had the privilege of nagging her to do her homework and telling her no, she couldn't pierce her tongue.

"If you really need Saturday," Don said, "we can stay home."

Susan waved her hand. "No. It's all right."

"If you have plans—"

"I already told you. I don't have any plans. Go."

As soon as she said the words, she gritted her teeth with irritation. She'd spent sixteen years of marriage giving in. She'd learned that behavior from her non-assertive mother, who saw nothing healthy about the expression of emotion and would turn herself inside out to avoid a fight, which was probably the reason she had high blood pressure and a stomach full of ulcers. Susan had never wanted to be like her, and to this day she didn't know quite how it had happened. How ironic was it that the one time Susan had jumped into a confrontation with both feet, she'd gotten arrested for it?

"Hi, Susan. How are you?"

Susan looked up to see Marla inching her way down the bench to sit next to Don. She smiled, that perfect, glowing smile that was more genuine than the Hope Diamond. She wasn't exactly beautiful, but she had that helpless feminine thing going on that made men fall all over her. How she'd decided Don was the one, Susan would never know.

They exchanged a few pleasantries that only made Susan feel worse, so she was glad when she heard the buzzer signaling the start of the game.

Don and Marla stood up. "We're going to sit closer to the court," he said, and Susan knew it was because he wanted to be able to yell along with the other fathers in that annoying way men did, as if their junior high daughters were playing in the championship game of the NCAA tournament. Susan also had the terrible feeling that Don wanted to sit down there with the other men because he was with a woman like Marla.

As they walked hand in hand down the bleachers,

it occurred to Susan that just once she would love to be the kind of woman men couldn't take their eyes off of. Actually, not all men. One man would do. Just one, before she got so old and decrepit that the very idea of it was laughable.

Then she looked down at her jeans, her sweatshirt, her tennis shoes and her oversized, utilitarian mom purse, and she was overcome by the most terrible feeling that happily ever after was never going to happen. Getting by ever after was going to have to do.

CHAPTER 5

The following Monday, Susan hurried from the hospital to class and managed to slip into her seat with a whole minute to spare. Tonya and Monica were already there. Danforth was planted in his chair, too, looking as if he'd been prepared to get out the paddle if she hadn't made it on time.

"Today we're going to talk about the physiology versus the psychology of anger," Danforth said. "Physiologically speaking, the amygdala is the part of the brain responsible for identifying threats and then sending out an alarm that causes us to react in order to protect ourselves. It sends that distress signal so rapidly, however, that the cortex, the part of the brain responsible for the application of thought and judgment, is unable to discern the rationality of our reaction."

"Huh?" Tonya said.

Susan leaned toward her. "If we're threatened, our brains are designed to react first and think later."

"Precisely," Danforth said.

Susan furtively rolled her eyes. If she'd said it so precisely, why hadn't he?

He droned on about how they had to teach their prefrontal cortex to judge the consequences of the proposed action of their amygdalas. Susan was a nurse. Physiology was her thing. And still she was bored to tears. She could only imagine how much the other women wished they were anywhere else.

Then Danforth started in on the psychology of anger, with special emphasis on the differences in the way men and women express their anger. After what seemed like forever, he put that set of notes away and pulled out something else.

"Now that we understand the psychology and physiology of anger," he said, "I'd like you ladies to learn a method by which you can express your anger constructively to the person with whom you're angry. It's known as the 'I-Message.'"

Sounded like psychobabble to Susan, but what the hell.

He handed them each a sheet of paper. "I want you to think about a situation that has angered you in the past and fill in these blanks."

Susan took a pen from her purse and looked at the form. The first line read, "I feel (be specific)." The second one read, "When you (give details of the behavior or circumstance)." The third line read, "Because (this is the *why* of your anger)."

They each filled in their forms, and a few minutes later Danforth said, "Ms. Saltzman. To whom is your I-Message directed?"

"My cousin, Sandra."

"Read it, please, phrasing your statement as if you're talking directly to her."

Monica sat up straighter in her chair. "I get angry…"

"Yes?"

"When you call from New York at three in the morning to cry on my shoulder about all your problems…"

"Because?" Danforth prompted.

"Because I don't like getting awakened from a sound sleep in the middle of the night."

"Hmm. Would you be this angry with anyone else who woke you at 3:00 a.m.?"

"Of course."

"Even if it were an emergency of some sort?"

"Well, no—"

"When she calls, what else do you discuss besides her problems?"

"Nothing, of course. It's all about her. On, and on, and on. She couldn't care less about anything going on in *my* life."

"Ah. Then your I-Message statement would more accurately read, 'I feel hurt when you call and monopolize the conversation to vent about your problems because it makes me feel as if you don't care about mine.'"

"Sorry, no," Monica said. "I've never cared whether she cares about me or not. It's those middle-of-the-night calls I can do without."

"In any case, you should discuss these phone calls with her in a nonconfrontational manner." He gave her a pointed stare. "But do try to be true to yourself about what lies at the root of your anger."

By the look on her face, Monica clearly thought she was right down at the very tip of that root, no matter what Danforth said.

He turned to Susan. "Ms. Roth? To whom is your I-Message directed?"

"My daughter. She's fourteen."

"Please read it for the class."

"I feel angry when you bring notes home from school but don't tell me about them until the last minute because then I'm rushed to complete whatever task I've been asked to do." Susan looked up. "It's no fun making brownies at midnight."

"Simple solution," Tonya said. "If she can't get you the note in time, she doesn't get the brownies."

"Right. And then all the other mothers think I'm a slacker."

Danforth tapped his chin with his index finger. "So the opinions of the other mothers are part of the reason you're angry? You feel inadequate?"

"No," Susan said. "I just want my daughter to give

me the notes so I have time to do whatever I'm supposed to do. That's all."

"So time pressure is another part of the equation."

"It wouldn't be," Susan said carefully, "if my daughter just *gave me the notes*."

"Restructured, your I-Message might read, 'I feel angry when you don't give me notes in time because then I have to accomplish the task on short notice or risk alienation from my peers.'"

Alienation from her peers? Did anyone besides Danforth actually talk like that?

"You see," he went on, "I sense that the problem doesn't lie with your daughter, but with your resentment over having to do these tasks at all."

"No, I really don't think—"

"Dig deep, Ms. Roth. Get at the real reason for your anger. Only by doing that will you be able to manage it effectively."

He was dead wrong about this. Susan didn't mind doing mom tasks. But she minded very much doing them at midnight, and that was about as deep as she intended to dig.

Danforth turned to Tonya. "Ms. Rutherford. To whom are you addressing your I-Message?"

"One of my customers."

"Share it with the class, please."

Tonya picked up her form and read. "I feel frustrated when you come into my shop with a horrible comb-over and expect me to cut it like that again."

Susan and Monica snickered a little, and Danforth held up his hand to them. "Because?"

"Because then you go back to work or wherever and somebody says, 'Hey, where did you get that...uh...great haircut?' and you say, 'Tonya Rutherford over at Tonya's Hair Design did it.' Then my reputation is in the toilet because everyone thinks I suggested that god-awful cut. Bad word of mouth can screw up my business something awful. But I can't say anything because pissing you off as a customer would screw up my business, too." She sat back and folded her arms. "So basically, I'm screwed."

Danforth blinked dumbly. "Yes. Well. At least you seem to be in touch with the reason for your anger in this situation." He cleared his throat. "Perhaps instead of direct confrontation, you could suggest a new haircut to this gentleman?"

"Please. Like I haven't tried that?"

"Hmm. Sometimes there are professional situations where confrontation, even constructive confrontation, isn't the answer. Could you simply be unavailable in the future when he makes an appointment?"

"I take walk-ins. What am I supposed to do? Lock the door when I see him coming?"

"You'll simply have to decide whether refusing to cut his hair if he refuses to change his style would be more helpful to your business than harmful."

"Did I mention he tips really well? I don't like losing good tippers. But that hair…*God*."

"In future classes, we'll be discussing how to manage the anger you're forced to hold inside when the expression of it is inappropriate. I'm certain that will help with your dilemma."

"Oh, screw it," Tonya said, waving her hand. "Next time he comes in, I'll just shave him bald."

Danforth closed his eyes. Was he counting to ten, maybe?

"You know that kind of aggressiveness is completely inappropriate," he said, as if Tonya would actually consider it.

Then again, maybe she would.

After that, Danforth turned on a video that showed people in a class like theirs sharing their I-Messages, as if they needed reinforcement on that particular method. By the time he finally dismissed class, Susan was more than ready to leave. She stopped by the bathroom on the way out, joined by Monica and Tonya.

"Thank God," Tonya said, as they stood at the sink. "One more class behind us. All that 'I-Message' stuff was a crock."

"I could have done without it, too," Monica said.

"Dig deeper," Susan said. "Why? As if I wasn't angry enough about the issue already?"

"After all that, I still don't know what to do about

Comb-over Guy." Tonya swiped on some lipstick. "I'm heading to that new bar and grill down the street for a drink. Anybody care to join me?"

"What's the atmosphere?" Monica asked. "Is it up-scale?"

"Haven't got a clue," Tonya said, stuffing her lipstick back into her purse, "but I'm betting if you pay them six bucks, they'll put a martini in front of you. So are you coming?"

"Sure," Monica said. "I could use a martini. Or, after that class, three." She turned to Susan. "How about you?"

"I don't know. My daughter's home alone."

"She's fourteen," Tonya said. "By the time I was fourteen, I was drinking martinis myself."

Susan decided it would be okay if she stayed for just a few minutes. Have one drink, then head home. She pulled out her cell phone and called Lani, who told her that of *course* she could stay home by herself, all night long if she had to, and to please stop treating her like a kid. Susan told her to make sure the doors were all locked, to finish her homework and to stay off the Internet.

By the time Susan clicked her phone shut, she could already taste that martini.

Fireside Bar & Grill was one of those places with lots of dark wood and brass, the kind of decor that made you feel as if you were in your father's study— back when fathers had studies. The crowd was older and the music dull, but all in all it was a cozy place with generous martinis, and after a few minutes Susan felt a pleasant little buzz that took the edge off the irritation she'd felt in class.

Tonya lit a cigarette and took a hard drag. "You know, I've had it with Danforth. And it's not anything in particular. It's everything in general. The way he walks. The way he talks. The words he uses. The clothes he wears. That great big nose."

"There isn't anything you like about the guy?" Monica asked.

Tonya paused, looking contemplative. Finally she shook her head. "Nope."

"Did you hear that comment he made about how men generally express anger more directly than women?" Susan asked.

"Guess we're the exceptions," Monica said.

"He said that when men murder, they usually shoot or stab. Women haul out the poison."

"I have to think there's something wrong with a man who feels superior about the way his gender kills people," Monica said.

"Or maybe he's trying to tell us to be *more* insidious," Susan said. "That way we might not end up in jail."

"I think the man/woman violence thing is all bullshit," Tonya said. "Personally, I like the direct approach. If I'd had a few dishes with me tonight, Danforth would have found out exactly *how* direct."

"Tonya, dear," Monica said. "It's an anger management class. Hurling things at the instructor is discouraged."

"Oh, yeah? Anger management? I've got news for you. I already know how to manage my anger. I'm CEO over my anger. I tell it to jump, it asks how high." She took a haughty drag on her cigarette and blew out the smoke. "My anger deserves to be freakin' employee of the year."

Susan had always wondered about women who seemed to have no fear. It generally meant they had even more fear than everybody else, but they were just good at hiding it. Susan had a feeling that Tonya was hiding more than most.

"So your own husband actually filed charges against you for assault?" Susan asked.

"Yep. I told him it was a really wussy thing to do, considering he's six-three, two-twenty and a firefighter to boot."

"And even *he's* afraid to mess with you?"

"Honey," Tonya said with a smug smile, "*everybody's* afraid to mess with me."

Susan had to hand it to Tonya. At least on the surface she had some sense of how to stand up for herself and take no crap. Susan's whole life had been about taking crap. Piling it up, sorting it out and, in general, dealing with it the way other people dealt with junk in their garage. Most of the time it wasn't even her own personal crap but her ex-husband's, her daughter's, her friends', even total strangers'.

"A firefighter," Monica said. "My, that conjures up all kinds of sexy thoughts, doesn't it?"

"Right," Tonya said. "That's because you're picturing nothing but hunky guys hauling around big, thick fire hoses and rescuing people from burning buildings." She snorted. "Too bad women never see all the sports talk and ball scratching that goes on around the station house. That'd cure them in a hurry."

Susan turned to Monica. "I would have thought you'd go for the corporate type."

"Sure, if I'm looking for a man to employ me, or maybe do my taxes. Otherwise, my prehistoric roots pop up every time. I think it's wired into our DNA."

Susan thought maybe evolution had affected her a little differently from Monica. Forget the chest-beating types. The attractive boy-next-door always had her at hello, which was why she'd been attracted to Don. But, as she'd discovered, looks weren't everything.

"Speaking of prehistoric roots," Susan said, "I think back to how I had my hand on Dennis's throat, and I can't believe I actually did it. Maybe that's wired into my DNA, too." She shook her head. "It felt so weird, like I was watching somebody else do it."

"I felt the same way," Monica said. "Throwing that flowerpot through that windshield felt like some kind of out-of-body experience. Like I was watching myself do something I was sure to regret, but I couldn't seem to stop myself."

They both turned to look at Tonya. "So how did it feel to go off on your husband?" Susan asked.

"He cheated," Tonya said, "so he deserved it."

She turned away when she said it, and Susan had a feeling it wasn't as simple as that.

Monica turned to Susan. "Did your husband cheat? Is that why you're divorced?"

"No."

"Did you fight a lot?"

"Actually, we might have worked things out over the years if we had, but both of us had a problem with confrontation. It was amazing we ever confronted each other long enough to get a divorce." She sighed. "Sometimes I wonder, though, if it was the best thing for our daughter."

"What?" Monica said. "To live in a house where icicles aren't hanging off the ceiling?"

"The divorce has been hard on her. She just isn't as happy as she used to be."

"You said she's fourteen," Tonya said. "Fourteen-year-old girls are never happy. They're bitchy, bad-tempered and annoying. At least I was." She smiled. "Come to think of it, I still am."

Susan sighed. "Great. I was hoping she'd outgrow it."

"She will," Tonya said, "but you're in for a hell of a ride until she does."

As she imagined a few more years of sulking and door slamming, Susan drained half her martini in one gulp. Then she turned to Monica. "So how's the job-hunt going?"

"The market is tight," she replied, "but I'll find something."

"How long can you survive without a job?" Tonya asked.

"A while longer. Ramen noodles are vastly under-rated. And if gas prices keep going up, there's always public transportation."

Her sarcasm wasn't lost on Susan. Ramen noodles tasted like wet cardboard, and Monica didn't seem like the type who would ever consider trading in her car for a monthly bus pass.

"Is it the reference from your old boss that's the problem?" Tonya asked. "Is he out to get you?"

Monica stared straight ahead. "Actually, no. I never get to the reference stage. As it turns out, there's a qual-ification I seem to be lacking."

"What's that?" Tonya asked.

"Youth."

Susan sat back, stunned. "You've got to be kidding. Age discrimination? Do you have any evidence of that?"

"No. But I know it's happening."

"That's crazy," Susan said. "The older you are, the more experience you have. Isn't that what they want?"

"Men in power want young, gorgeous women

around them, whether it's their wives or their assistants. Those are the only qualifications necessary."

"You should sue," Tonya said. "I bet you could make it stick, too."

"No, thank you," Monica said. "The last thing I would want to be is the poor geriatric woman bringing that lawsuit."

She drained her martini, set the glass on the table and signaled the waitress to bring her another one.

"Is there some other kind of job out there you can do?" Susan asked.

"Well, one of the department stores is looking for perfume representatives."

"Selling perfume? That doesn't sound so bad."

"No. It's more like…marketing."

"Marketing is good."

"Yes. It's wonderful. You take one of those little cards, squirt perfume on it, then shove it at some unsuspecting woman walking through the cosmetics department who wishes you'd go away."

Susan winced. She'd had a few of those little cards shoved at her, and she'd certainly never envied the woman doing the shoving.

"If all I can make is minimum wage," Monica went on, "I might as well save time and effort and head straight to a cardboard box down by the Trinity River."

The first time Susan saw Monica, she had looked pristine and perfect, surrounded by an aura of compo-

sure and confidence that said she had it all together.
Right now, though, there was a crack in that aura, with
more than a little uncertainty leaking out. Susan could
never have imagined it, but she actually felt sorry for
her.

"How would you feel about working in a hospital?"
she asked Monica.

Monica's nose crinkled. "Around all those sick
people?"

"It's an administrative job."

"Doing what?"

"One of the department heads is looking for an assistant."

"Oh, yeah? What does it pay?"

"I don't know, but whatever it is it'll keep you out
of that cardboard box."

"Can you get me an interview?"

Susan shrugged. "Sure. I'll even put in a good word
for you. Come to the hospital tomorrow and I'll take
you to the human resources department to fill out an
application. They'll take it from there."

"So which department head is looking for an assistant?"

"The director of nursing."

Monica froze. "Is that a woman?"

"Yes. Andi Shaunessy. That's Andi with an *i*. Is that
a problem?"

"I just tend to get along better with men."

Susan shrugged. "If you'd rather not apply—"

"No. I need a job." Monica took a sip of her drink. Then a bigger sip. She set the glass back down on the table. "It's no big deal. I can work for a woman."

But something about Monica's manner told Susan it was a very big deal, though she didn't know why. By the worried look on her face, her situation was probably even worse than she was letting on. Because of that, Susan was relieved Monica hadn't asked more details about the particular woman she'd be working for. What she didn't know right now wouldn't hurt her, but it might keep her from being in the running for a job she desperately needed.

As Susan lifted her glass and clinked the other women's, toasting to Monica's job-hunting success, she decided she was going to think positively. This time tomorrow, Monica was going to be employed, which would give her something even more to celebrate. Unless, of course, she was searching for yet another flowerpot, and this time Susan would be her target.

CHAPTER 6

The next afternoon, Monica met Susan in the E.R. and they walked upstairs to the human resources department. Monica hated the way a hospital smelled, and she couldn't shake the image of unseen germs crawling on every surface.

They entered the small suite of offices on the second floor. Everything there was clean and neat and utilitarian, which seemed to be the hospital's standard decor. Apparently, plush carpet, cherrywood and fine art harbored more of those unseen germs than tile floors, laminate and motivational posters.

Susan leaned over to peek into an office. "Marsha's not here," she said. "But it's not quite two o'clock yet."

"Susan. Hello."

Monica turned around to see a man standing at another office door. He was tall, probably late forties, with sandy-brown hair, green eyes and *nice guy* written all over him. Beside his door was a nameplate that read *Paul White, Director of Human Resources*.

He smiled at Susan. "What brings you up here?"

"This is my friend, Monica Saltzman. She's applying for the job as Andi's assistant. I talked to Marsha about it this morning."

"Marsha took a late lunch, but she's due back anytime." He held out his hand to Monica. "Paul White."

She gave him a brilliant smile. "Monica Saltzman. It's a pleasure."

Nice grip. Friendly smile. No wedding ring. She filed away his name and job title for future reference. It never hurt to have her mental Rolodex spinning all the time.

"I already put in a good word for her with Andi," Susan said.

Paul nodded, then turned to Monica. "You're in luck. I think you're the first person Andi is interviewing for the job."

The phone rang inside his office.

"I need to get that. It's nice to meet you, Monica. And it's good to see you, Susan."

Susan smiled and nodded. When Paul disappeared into his office, Monica turned to Susan.

"I really appreciate this, you know. I have to find a job, and with your recommendation—" She stopped short. "Susan? What's the matter?"

"What do you mean?"

"I don't know. You look sick. Your cheeks are all red."

Susan put her hand to her face. "They are? Uh…maybe I'm coming down with something. I thought maybe this morning I might be…you know. Getting a fever."

Just then Marsha came back into the office. Susan quickly introduced Monica to her, then headed for the door.

"I'd better go downstairs and take my temperature," she said. "Good luck with the job interview. Be sure to let me know what happens, okay?"

"I will."

Monica followed Marsha into her office, where she went through the standard application process, and for the first time in a long time, she actually had hope. The director seemed to like Susan, which meant she probably had a good reputation at the hospital, which meant a recommendation from her would go a long way. With luck, in just a few hours Monica would be gainfully employed again.

Susan strode down the hall to the ladies' room, shoved open the door and went straight for the sink. Her face still felt hot, and when she looked at herself in the mirror it was just as Monica had said. Her cheeks looked as if she'd been sitting two feet from a blazing campfire.

She turned on the cold water and splashed some on her face before wiping it with a paper towel. She took a deep breath to calm her racing heart, feeling as if she were sixteen all over again and the boy she had a crush on two lockers down had just said hello.

It had been a long time since she'd looked at a man as something more than a friend, a relative or a husband, but whenever Paul so much as walked into the same room with her, her body reacted in ways she couldn't control and her thoughts went to places they hadn't been in years.

The hospital grapevine had told her he was divorced, he'd come from another hospital to take this job and he was still single. Her own reaction to him told her he was an attractive man she wanted to get to know better. Unfortunately, she didn't have the first idea how to go about it.

Because she was bringing Monica up to Human Resources today, she'd known it was possible that she might see Paul, so she'd spent a little more time that morning in front of the mirror. She'd blown her hair dry to give it some extra fluff, then put on some blush and a swipe of lipstick. By her reflection now, though, she looked just as she always did—plain and functional, the kind of woman most men didn't even realize was in the room.

In the three months Paul had worked at the hospital, he'd always been pleasant to her whenever he saw her, even stopping to talk now and then, and for a while Susan had hoped that meant something. But as time went on, she realized she was nothing special to him, that he was like that with everyone.

When she'd been hauled off by the police that day,

she'd been mortified at the thought of Paul hearing all about it. Of course he would; it was a personnel issue. She'd gone behind closed doors with him and Andi and told her side of the story, emphasizing how much she loved her job and that she didn't want to lose it. Paul had actually smiled at her and told her not to worry about it, that her position was perfectly safe and always would be. And that was the day her attraction had turned into a full-fledged infatuation.

Give it up. He'll never notice you. Not the way you want him to.

She left the bathroom and headed back down to the ER, where she spent the next hour catching up on patient charts and wishing dreams really did come true.

The next morning, Monica sat waiting for her interview, nervousness creeping through her at the thought of talking to a woman about a job. What possible advantage could she hope to have there? And when she'd found out yesterday what the salary was, she'd wondered if it would even pay her bills. But she had to remember that some money beat no money, and she was going to do whatever she could to get the job, which always included looking her best. She had decided to wear a pantsuit in a pretty coral-pink, which really wasn't her shade, but maybe a girly color might help her bond with another woman.

Okay. Change of paradigm. Think sisterhood. You're

bound to have something in common with her. Find out
what it is and exploit it.

Suddenly, a door swung open and a woman appeared. Until that moment, Monica wouldn't have believed that Wal-Mart actually sold clothes in ultra-petite 2X. The woman had short dark hair that looked as if she'd cut it herself, and it was quite possible that not a speck of makeup had ever touched her face.

So much for having something in common.

"You Monica?" she said.

Monica stood up. "Yes. I have an appointment with Andi Shaunessy at two o'clock."

"That's me. Come on in."

Monica had hoped this woman was the substitute director of nursing sitting in for the lovely and stylish Andi Shaunessy, a woman with whom she could compare shopping trips and spa treatments.

No such luck.

Andi circled her desk to sit behind it. Monica took a seat, trying to put a pleasant look on her face, but the deadpan stare the woman gave her in return told her there was no way on earth this could possibly go well.

Andi glanced at her application, then tossed it down on her desk. "Tell me what you did on your last job."

Monica wasn't sure where to start, even though she didn't have much to choose from. "Well," she began, "I kept my boss's calendar. I'm a very organized person, and he always complimented me on—"

"I keep my own calendar. What else?"

"Oh. Uh…well, whenever he had a lunch meeting, I made sure everything was in order. I know the names of several restaurants that cater—"

"I don't do business over lunch. Gives me indigestion. Keep going."

Monica felt light-headed. "I'm very efficient with travel arrangements. I know where all the best bargains are. There's one agent in particular I know who—"

"My job doesn't require travel."

Oh, God. What else? Think! She cleared her throat. "Basically…well, I suppose you could say that whatever my boss needed, I made sure he had it."

Andi settled back in her chair, leaning sideways on the armrest, those sharp little eyes skewering Monica like bayonets. "So basically you were a desk ornament who kissed a lot of ass."

Monica swallowed hard, trying to come up with an argument for that. She couldn't.

"Says here you type fifty," Andi said. "Is that right?"

"Yes." More or less. Mostly less.

"This is a small hospital," Andi said. "We don't have much state-of-the-art equipment when it comes to office machines. If you can run a plain old telephone, a fax machine, copier, a computer and a coffeepot, that's all I'm looking for."

"Yes. Of course."

"What computer programs do you know?"

"Word, and some Excel, and maybe a little bit of—"

"Those'll do." Andi leaned forward, folding her hands on her desk. "This job isn't brain surgery. Just standard office stuff. Do you think you can handle that?"

"Yes. Of course."

"You ever work for a woman before?"

"Uh…no. I haven't."

"You got anything *against* working for a woman?"

Yes! "No. Nothing at all."

"Do you drink?"

"Only socially."

"Do drugs?"

"Of course not."

"Have any husband or boyfriend problems you're gonna end up bringing to work with you?"

Monica blinked. "Excuse me, but…can you ask those questions in a job interview?"

"Would you rather leave the answers to my imagination?"

"Uh…no. I don't even have a husband or a boyfriend."

Andi sat back again, giving her a hard stare. "Seems to me that the best thing you've got going for you is that Susan recommended you. I like Susan. Susan works hard. I'll go out on a limb for Susan. Do you get my drift?"

"Uh…yeah."

"And I imagine you'd never want to do anything to disappoint Susan, would you?"

"No. Of course not."

"I was a Navy nurse. I don't tolerate people who are late, sloppy or disrespectful. Are we clear on that?"

"Yes, ma'am."

"Okay, then. You're hired. I'll call Human Resources. Go back up there and fill out the appropriate paperwork. Then be back here tomorrow at oh-eight-hundred."

Monica felt pretty sure her mouth was hanging open, but she felt completely and utterly unable to close it. Finally, she rose from the chair and started to leave the office.

"And, Monica?"

She turned back. "Yes?"

Andi leaned over and looked at her from the ground up. "Nice polish on the shoes. Sharp crease in the pants. I like that."

Monica smiled. "Thank you."

"But the pink..." She frowned, shaking her head. "Now, I do have a real soft spot in my heart for navy blue. You think about that on your next trip to Neiman Marcus, you hear?"

"Yes, ma'am."

Monica just stood there, wondering if any more volleys were coming her way.

"You can go now," Andi said.

"Yes, ma'am."

Monica left the office, walked partway down the hall, then stopped and leaned against the wall, breathing suddenly a chore.

What the *hell* had just happened in there?

Susan. She had to talk to Susan.

Monica turned down one hall after another until she got to the emergency room, where she found Susan sitting in a glassed-in area. She knocked on the glass and motioned for her to come out. In the meantime, she sank to a nearby bench, sure she was going to be sick.

A few moments later, Susan sat down beside her. "Uh…you don't look so good. Should I have brought a barf basin?"

"For God's sake, Susan! You didn't tell me she was Nazi Nurse!"

Susan held up her palm. "Okay, I know she can be a little brusque, but—"

"A little brusque? Adolph Hitler was a *pussycat* compared to Andi Shaunessy!"

"So you didn't get the job?"

"Yes! I got the job! That's what scares me!" Monica slumped against the wall, squeezing her eyes closed. "Oh, God. This is never going to work out."

"Did I hear you say you're going to be working for Andi?"

Monica looked up to see a large, sour-faced woman in blue scrubs staring down at her.

"She's Andi's new assistant," Susan said.

The woman grinned. "Oh, yeah? Hope she put in for combat pay."

"Evie—"

"Does she know what Andi did to her last assistant?" Monica slid her hand to her throat. "What?"

"Never mind," Evie said with a wave of her hand. "They haven't actually found the body, and they can't prosecute what they can't prove."

"Evie!" Susan said.

"Fair warning, sweetie," Evie said to Monica. "Better dust off your flak jacket. She's gonna be hitting you with both barrels."

As she walked off with a satisfied little snicker, Monica turned to Susan. "My God. Who was that horrible woman?"

"Evie Thomason. If there's trouble around here, she's behind it. Never forget that."

Great. Just what Monica needed in her life. More trouble.

"You're worrying too much," Susan said. "I know Andi is demanding, but if you do your job you're not going to have any trouble with her at all."

"She told me she was hiring me because you recommended me." Monica exhaled. "I'm not sure whether to thank you for that or not."

"Yes, you should thank me. And, now that you're employed, next week after class the martinis are on you."

And Monica was going to be drinking most of them.

"Susan? Uh, oh-eight-hundred would be...?"

Susan smiled. "That's 8:00 a.m." She patted her on the arm. "I gotta get back to work. See you in the morning."

In spite of all her apprehension, by two o'clock the next afternoon Monica was starting to believe that working for Andi might not be so bad after all. She sent Monica on various errands around the hospital, which made it easy for her to scope out the men in power around there. Andi hadn't asked her to type anything yet, and the copier was one of the older models without all the weird computerized stuff that made Monica's eyes cross. The coffeepot was standard issue, and, since there were only a couple of phone lines coming into the office, those were manageable, too. And whenever Andi was in her office, she had the door shut, which meant that most of the time Monica didn't even have to try to look busy.

"Well, hello."

She turned around to see a man standing over her desk. He was maybe thirty-five, tall and handsome with a glittering white smile. She returned his smile with one of her own, wondering who he might be. A doctor, maybe? Administrator? Relative of a patient?

"The view has certainly improved since the last time I was here," he said, with a fawningly insincere lilt to his voice. "Maybe I should drop by more often."

Salesman.

He raised his eyebrows. "And you are…?"

"Monica Saltzman. Ms. Shaunessy's new assistant."

"That's who I'm here to see," he said, heading toward Andi's office.

"But—"

"Don't worry. She's expecting me."

He gave Monica a wink as he knocked on the door. She heard something unintelligible inside Andi's office, and then the guy went in. Approximately ten seconds passed. Suddenly the door opened again, and the guy came back out with Andi in his wake. He walked right out the door without looking in Monica's direction or bothering to say a word.

Andi stopped in front of her desk, wearing that tight-jawed, military-ready expression, as if she was getting ready to rip a raw recruit in half.

"Monica."

She swallowed hard. "Yes?"

"Did that man have an appointment?"

"Uh…he told me you were expecting him."

"Wrong. He's a pharmaceutical salesman who just happened to be in the hospital and thought he'd stop by to annoy me. I forgot to mention something yesterday. One of your jobs is to make sure people stay on the other side of my door unless they have a real good reason to pass through it. I copy my daily agenda for you every morning for a reason. Somebody shows up, you look at that. If they've got an appointment, you let 'em in. If not, you boot 'em to the curb."

She started to walk off, then turned back. "And when you're running errands for me, stop flirting with the doctors. They have better things to do and so do you."

"What? Flirting? I wasn't flirting. I just stopped to say hello to a few of them. You know. To introduce myself."

"Introductions take thirty seconds. When you're hanging around ten minutes later, that's a problem."

Monica was stunned. When had Andi seen her talking to anyone?

"I can see you're confused. That's good. Don't think you can put something past me. I've got intelligence sources in this hospital you can't even imagine. I send you on an errand, you complete that errand and get back here. And when you're here, you keep people out of my face who have no reason to be in it. Are we clear?"

Monica nodded.

"Now, come into my office. I have a report for you to copy and collate."

As Andi turned and walked away, Monica came very close to making a juvenile hand gesture, but since she wasn't entirely sure the woman didn't have eyes in the back of her head she figured she'd better not.

Okay. Since Big Sister was watching, Monica was going to have to stick closer to the office from now on, at least during work hours. The paycheck wasn't much, but right now it was all she had. But that didn't mean she couldn't spend her breaks and her lunch hour in the cafeteria or at the coffeehouse across the street, chatting with men in white coats. Andi couldn't object to her talking to people on her own time, now could she?

At two o'clock the next Monday, Susan had just finished checking out a toddler for the flu when somebody hollered at her to pick up the phone. She snagged the receiver and held it against her shoulder as she finished scribbling a note into the patient's chart.

"Hey, Lani. What's up?"

"Kaylee's having a party Friday night. Can I go?"

"I don't know. What kind of party is it?"

"Just a regular party."

"With boys?"

"What kind of a party would it be if boys weren't there?"

Three years ago, it had been, *What kind of party would it be if boys were there?*

"Will Kaylee's parents be there?"

"Uh...I think they're going out. But Kaylee says they'll be home later."

"How much later?"

"Not very."

Well, that was specific. And even when Kaylee's parents were there, they didn't know what discipline was. It would be just like them to show up *after* the drugs were consumed and two girls got pregnant.

"I'd really rather you not go to a party at Kaylee's house. Particularly under those circumstances."

"But, Mom—"

"Can we talk about this tonight?"

"You have class tonight and won't be home until late. Kaylee's calling me, wanting to know if I can come."

"I don't think it's a good idea."

"Why not?"

"You know I don't like you going to friends' houses when their parents aren't home."

"Mom, I'm fourteen years old!"

Susan couldn't imagine why Lani thought that bringing up the fact that she was four long years away from adulthood was going to help her case.

"Dad already said I could go."

"He *what?*"

"He said it was all right with him but I'd have to ask you."

It was all Susan could do not to make a beeline to Don's office and smack him senseless. Once again, Dad got to be the good guy. *You want to go away with your eighteen-year-old boyfriend for the weekend? Sounds like fun. Smoke pot? No problem. Get a tattoo? Why, sure. But you know your mom…*

"I need to know *now*," Lani said.

"The answer is no."

"Mom, you're being unreasonable!"

"Okay. I'm being unreasonable. But you're still not going to that party."

"But I have to! Everyone is going to be there!"

Which only meant that "Everyone's" parents weren't doing their jobs.

"If Dad says I can go, I don't see why I can't."

"Because you're not living with your father. You're living with me. So what I say goes."

"Then maybe I'll go live with Dad!"

Susan almost laughed out loud. She could just see the look on Don's face at the prospect of his fourteen-year-old daughter living in his middle-aged bachelor pad. All that spontaneous sex would fly right out the window.

"I have to go, Lani. I'll see you at home later."

"But, Mom—"

"Goodbye."

She hung up the phone over Lani's protests, her anger growing exponentially with every breath. How could Don *do* this to her?

"Bad news?"

Susan turned to see her friend Carl standing behind her, wearing purple scrubs, with a tiny stuffed monkey clipped to the stethoscope hanging around his neck.

"That's about the only kind I seem to get these days," Susan said.

"You know," Carl said, as he circled the desk and tossed down a chart, "sometimes I think it would be great to be a father, and then I catch the other end of a conversation like that and I thank God for the single life. What's Miss Lani's problem today?"

"She wants to go to a party Friday night. This girl's parents are about as responsible as college freshmen on homecoming weekend. And I'm *so* unreasonable for telling her she can't go. And get this. She asked Don first. He told her it was fine with him, but she'd have to check with me."

Carl shook his head. "Does that man have any balls at all?"

"None that I can tell."

"You're doing the right thing, Susan. You've got to lay down the law with kids, or they'll walk all over you. Trust me, I know. My parents lived with dusty footprints from head to toe."

Susan smiled. "You know, maybe you should reconsider being a father. You're up on all the stuff kids try to pull. It'd be like a burglar becoming a cop. Think of the advantage you'd have."

"Sorry. I have no desire to be a single parent, and the men I date aren't exactly into parenthood."

"That's because they're barely out of childhood themselves."

Carl drew back with mock offense. "Are you suggesting I'm a cradle robber?"

"Well…"

"I *am*, of course. I just wondered if that was what you were suggesting."

Susan smiled. Carl was thirty-eight, but he had a thing for younger men. If they weren't in their twenties, he wasn't interested. At a time in her life where Susan felt as if she was over the hill and wanted to hide behind something most of the time, Carl blasted through life with the kind of self-confidence she could only imagine.

In the first few weeks after she and Don had split up, Carl had been the one person who could shake her out of her depression. He'd told her again and again that her life wasn't over, that it was just beginning. Even though she hadn't seen any solid evidence of that in the past year and a half, she had still appreciated the pep talks.

"Carl? I have an idea. I'm divorced, and you're not seeing anyone right now. Why don't you and I run off together?"

"Hmm. I have to say we're compatible, but there is that sex thing."

"Come on, now. Sex really isn't all that important, is it?"

Carl grinned. "Speak for yourself, Susan." He patted her on the shoulder. "I'll tell you what. The moment Mother Nature stops shoving this gay thing on me, it's you and me forever."

As he walked away, Susan sighed. Why were the

straight men like Don and the gay ones like Carl? What kind of twisted setup was that?

Then she thought about Paul.

She'd seen him in the cafeteria at lunch today, and she'd almost worked up the nerve to ask him if she could join him, then veered away at the last minute. *Tomorrow,* she'd told herself. *You can do it tomorrow.*

But she was afraid that where her love life was concerned, tomorrow was never going to come.

CHAPTER 7

"Tonight we're going to be talking about the nature of anger," Danforth said that evening, kicking off class number three. "We always think of anger as being a singular emotion that can exist on its own, but in truth it's a secondary emotion that follows a primary one. If one focuses only on the secondary emotion, the anger, one never gets to the heart of the problem."

Danforth had begun his lecture at precisely seven o'clock, because God forbid he miss one minute of bestowing his dazzling brain power on his students. Susan didn't even try to figure out what the hell he was saying. She just wanted to doodle on her notepad for the next two hours and tune him out completely. As he prattled on, she found herself thinking this would be a really good time to have a stroke and slip into a coma.

Susan glanced at the other women, who were just as enthralled as she was. Tonya sat with her arms folded and her legs crossed, dangling her shoe off her toe and bobbing it up and down as she inspected her manicure while Monica emitted an occasional sigh of sheer boredom as she stared out the window.

"We may feel unloved or attacked or disrespected," Danforth said, "and if that emotion becomes intense enough, we read it as anger. For instance...Ms. Roth?"

Susan jolted out of her half-awake state. "Yes?"

"Right before you attacked that man, what emotion were you feeling?"

She started to say anger, but clearly that wasn't what he wanted to hear. She shrugged. "Irritation, I suppose. And frustration. He wouldn't leave me alone."

"Why was it so irritating and frustrating? Most women enjoy attention from a man."

Tonya screwed up her face. "Did you not hear her describe the guy? He wasn't her type. He wasn't *any* woman's type."

"That's right," Susan said. "And I was having such an awful day already—"

"Ah. So there were precursory incidents. Please share those with the class."

In that moment, Susan would have paid Danforth a hundred bucks never to use words like *precursory* again.

"My daughter was having problems that morning. I was late to work." She winced at the memory. "And I'd just found out my ex-husband was getting married."

Danforth stroked his chin. "How did that make you feel?"

"I didn't expect him to stay single forever."

"That's not what I asked. I asked how it made you feel to find out your ex-husband was remarrying."

"I wasn't angry with him, if that's what you're after. Not really. I mean, I suppose it would have been nice if at least he'd told me before he told our daughter, but she was the one who was upset about it."

"Did your husband leave you, or was it the other way around?"

"It was mutual."

"Who moved out? You or him?"

"He did. There was our daughter to think about, and the house—"

"Exactly. Your husband left you, which was a psychologically damaging incident. Then that morning you discovered that he'd found a wife to replace you. Your negative emotions about that escalated, and the moment you found an outlet for the resultant anger, you snapped."

Speaking of negative emotions, Susan was having a few right now. "That's not how it happened."

"It is paramount that we look deeper for the causes of our behavior, Ms. Roth. The issue is never the issue."

"Maybe it is," Monica said. "Susan was probably handling the news about her husband just fine. It was the problem she was having with that intrusive little geek that ticked her off."

"But again," Danforth said, "anger is a secondary emotion that always has an underlying cause."

"Okay," Tonya said. "Suppose I'm walking down the street. Some bozo isn't watching where he's going, and he runs right in to me. I get mad, and we exchange a few words. What's the underlying emotion there?"

"The average woman wouldn't get angry about such a thing. She would take into account the fact that people are fallible and occasionally don't watch where they're going."

"For the sake of argument, let's assume I *do* get angry about it. What underlying emotion are we talking about?"

"A veritable host of them, I'd say, given the overreaction to a relatively benign situation."

Tonya folded her arms. "Name three."

"Suspicion, hypersensitivity and intolerance," Danforth said, without missing a beat. "Suspicion about whether the incident was actually an accident, hypersensitivity about a stranger invading your personal space and intolerance of the mistakes other people make. It's the culmination of all those emotions that results in the secondary emotion of anger."

Tonya drew back. "Wow. And here all this time I thought I was just getting mad. Turns out I'm way deeper than I thought."

"Depth has little to do with it, Ms. Rutherford. It's merely an expression of the range of human emotions present in all people."

Tonya gave him a not-so-subtle up-yours look that seemed to go right over his head. Fortunately, that was the last of the student/teacher interaction for the evening because, when it got right down to it, what Danforth wanted to hear most was the sound of his own voice.

After class, Susan was glad when Tonya suggested they head to the Fireside Bar & Grill again, where a round of martinis was sure to take the edge off the boredom they'd experienced tonight.

"Danforth is so aggravating," Tonya said. "He goes digging for psychological crap that's not even there. I mean, look at how he went off on you, Susan."

Susan sighed. "Unfortunately, I think in my case he may be right."

"Right?" Tonya said. "Danforth? Please say it isn't so."

"It was like he said. I might not have gone off on Dennis if the rest of that stuff hadn't happened that day. It's just that…"

"What?"

Susan wasn't usually one to spill all her personal problems to other people, but she rarely had the opportunity to talk to other women who weren't associated with either her job or Lani's school. In spite of how different they all were, she felt an odd camaraderie with Tonya and Monica that she couldn't quite explain. She just had the feeling that what happened in anger management class stayed in anger management class.

Or in the bar they went to afterward, as the case may be.

"That morning," Susan went on, "all I could think about was that Don had moved right on past me and found a decent woman to marry, but I couldn't do any better than a guy like Dennis. And I thought…what if this is it? What if I'm destined to spend my life alone? Or worse, with a man and his Star Wars action figures?"

"Given those choices," Tonya said, "I think I'd go it alone."

"That's exactly how I feel now. Alone. And…I don't know. Invisible."

"What do you mean?" Monica asked.

She wasn't sure. She only knew that whatever it was she'd felt it for a long time, even before she and Don had divorced. That feeling that she was floating through life, as if she were barely a person. Just a cog in a wheel that was taken for granted as long as if was functioning the way it was supposed to, but that was about it.

Susan ran her finger up and down the stem of her glass. "To my daughter, I'm nothing but a cook and a maid and a taxi driver. To my ex-husband, I'm the nanny service for our daughter. At work, I'm this nameless, faceless person who keeps hearts beating and brains functioning. That's how I feel sometimes. As if my vital signs are there, but I'm not really living."

"While your ex-husband is living quite nicely," Monica said.

"Exactly."

"Well, at least there's an easy way to get over *that* feeling," Tonya said.

"What's that?"

"You need to get laid."

Susan closed her eyes. Were there any shades of gray in Tonya's mind? Any at all?

"When's the last time you went on a date?" she asked.

Susan wanted to hide under the table. "I think it's been...now, let me think...oh, yeah. Seventeen years."

Tonya slumped backward with total astonishment. "How long have you been divorced?"

"A year and a half."

"You mean to tell me you haven't had sex in a year and a half?"

"More like two. Those last six months with Don weren't so great."

"My God. No wonder you're so uptight. You need to get out there and start dating again."

"Believe it or not, that's a pretty big leap for me."

"Don didn't have any problem doing it," Monica pointed out.

"Yeah, and do you know why?" Susan said. "Because he doesn't have to be that cook, maid and taxi driver. He gets to play dad a couple of times a week and live it up with his fiancée the rest of the time. I'm the one left with all the responsibility."

"Still, you're going to have to make time for men,"

Tonya said. "You're not getting any younger, you know."

"Thanks, Tonya. I really needed to hear that."

"The older a man is, the younger he wants a woman to be. Just ask Monica."

Monica frowned. "Must you be so direct?"

"Just speaking the truth." Tonya turned to Susan. "So when do you think you might start dating again?

Susan shrugged. "I don't know. Maybe when Lani graduates."

"Didn't you say she was fourteen? God, Susan, by the time she's out of the house, your privates could shrivel up and fall off."

Now that was a lovely image to think about. Before Susan had simply felt in limbo. Now she felt as if she were sliding down that slippery slope of middle age, gliding right into her golden years. Only, at the rate she was going, there wasn't going to be anything golden about them.

"So how do you feel about the woman your ex is marrying?" Monica asked.

"Marla's very nice."

"Oh, please," Tonya said. "I'm not buying that."

"Actually, you're right. I misspoke. She's *extremely* nice. Sometimes I wish she was one of those bitchy women I could hate. That would sure make my life a lot easier."

"Is she younger than you?" Tonya asked.

"Second wives are always younger," Monica said. "It's the law."

Then her gaze drifted over to another table in the bar, and her eyes widened with surprise.

"Oh, God."

"What's wrong?" Susan asked.

Monica looked at her martini again, as if she wished she'd kept her mouth shut. "Nothing."

"No, something," Tonya said. "It's that guy in the suit who just came in, isn't it? Who is he?"

Monica's lips tightened. "My ex-boss. Jerry Womack."

Susan and Tonya craned their necks around.

"Hey!" Monica whispered. "Would you two mind being a little more subtle?"

"Who's he with?" Susan asked.

Monica all but snarled. "Nora O'Dell."

"Who is she?"

"The woman who works for Jerry now."

"The one who got the job he promised you?" Tonya said.

"That's right."

"You're kidding. It looks like he's taking the baby-sitter home and they stopped off for a drink."

Susan watched as they slid into a booth, both of them sitting on the same side.

"They sure do look cozy," she said.

"Of course they do," Monica said. "How do you think she got the job?"

"So she screwed her way into it, huh?" Tonya looked disgusted. "Well, you lucked out. Any boss who gives a woman a job in return for sex is a man you don't want to work for."

"No kidding," Susan said. "That's about as low as it gets."

"Can you imagine any woman who'd sleep with her boss in return for favors?" Tonya said.

Monica turned slowly to face Tonya. "Yes. I can imagine it."

For the count of three, Monica just stared at her. Then Tonya's face crumpled, and she dropped her forehead to her hand. "Oh, crap. *You* were sleeping with the boss."

It took Susan a moment or two to get the picture, and when she did she turned to Monica with a look of astonishment. "Wait a minute. Let me get this straight. You were sleeping with him while you were working for him, and then he dumped you to sleep with her and the job came along with it?"

Monica shrugged offhandedly. "That about sums it up."

"But why would you do that?" Susan asked. "Like you've got nothing else to offer?"

"Stop being naive. I discovered a long time ago that I got farther with my looks than with my brain. What's wrong with playing to my strengths?"

"Because looks fade. And then what do you have?"

"That's easy for you to say. You're obviously smart. You have a degree and a professional job." She turned to Tonya. "You have your own business. What do I have?"

"You could have gone to college," Susan said. "Why didn't you?"

"Please. I barely graduated from high school."

"Why?"

"Because I was beautiful, of course. What was the point of filling my mind up with all that useless knowledge?" She paused. "At least, that was what my mother always told me."

Monica acted as if that were no big deal, and maybe at one point in her life it hadn't been. A woman like her could subsist on her beauty for quite some time. But now her bravado seemed weak and hollow, and Susan could tell it masked all kinds of fears. How could a mother do that to her daughter? How could she tell her to stake her future on something so shallow and fleeting?

"You never should have listened to your mother," Susan said.

"It's not like she started telling me that yesterday," Monica said. "I heard it from the time I was five years old. Marry rich, she said. Well, that never happened. So when Jerry offered me a job making more than I ever had in my life, I took it."

"And the sex that came along with it?" Tonya said.

Monica frowned. "Yes, Tonya. And the sex that came along with it."

"But you have a good job now," Susan said. "And you didn't have to sleep your way into it."

"It's a job. But hardly a good one. I can't work for Andi forever."

"You're going to quit?"

"There are other opportunities at that hospital where I could make more money."

"Well, there's nothing wrong with moving up the ladder," Susan said. "Go for it."

"I said there were opportunities. I didn't say I'd be the best qualified candidate. What I need is somebody influential around there who would be willing to recommend me."

"What do you mean?" Susan asked.

"I'm betting if I get in good with the director of human resources, he can open all kinds of doors for me."

Susan's eyes widened. "What?"

"If I play my cards right," Monica went on, "Paul White will be wrapped around my finger before he knows what hit him."

CHAPTER 8

Susan felt as if Monica had knocked her right off her bar stool, leaving her flat on her back and gasping for air. "Paul White?"

"Sure. Can you imagine a better person to recommend me for jobs at the hospital than the director of human resources?"

Susan felt a stab of jealousy so sharp that she knew now what a kidney stone must feel like. The one man at that hospital Susan was interested in, and Monica was going to swoop in and grab him before she even had a chance to?

"A man like Paul isn't going to fall for that," Susan said.

"He won't be falling for anything. I just want to get to know him better. If he likes me, he might be willing to help me. What's so wrong with that?"

"So you don't intend to sleep with him?" Susan asked.

Monica met her gaze evenly. "It's hard to say exactly where a relationship might go."

"That's not a relationship. Not when one of the people involved has an ulterior motive."

"This may come as a shock to you, Susan, but the business world turns on ulterior motives."

"And I think that really stinks."

Monica set her drink down and eyed Susan suspiciously. "What's your problem?"

"I don't have a problem. You're the one with the problem. Sleeping with a man because you want something from him is a *problem*."

"I don't get this. Why the sudden chastising? When I told you I was sleeping with Jerry, it didn't bother you like this. So why are you—" She froze, and then a knowing look came over her face. "Ah."

"What?"

"You have a thing for him, don't you?"

Susan suddenly felt transparent, as if she were thirteen again and her sister was reading her diary. "Of course not."

"No," Monica said. "You do. Now I remember how you were looking at him that first day we were in H.R."

"Monica—"

"And once I saw you pass him in the hall. You stopped and watched him as he walked away. You couldn't take your eyes off him."

"I don't know what you're talking about."

"And you're afraid if I go after him you don't stand a chance."

"That's not true."

"What's not true? That you have a thing for him, or that you don't stand a chance?"

"Neither one!"

"If you like him, why don't you just say so?"

"I don't like him! Not like that!"

"Come on, Susan," Tonya said. "You might as well admit it. Even I can tell you're lying."

"I've heard enough of this." Susan grabbed her purse and threw a pair of tens onto the table. "You know, I really feel sorry for you, Monica. Any woman who thinks she has to sleep with a man to get ahead is pitiful."

"No more pitiful than a woman who doesn't sleep with men at all."

Stung by that remark, Susan felt tears burn behind her eyes. She opened her mouth to respond, but realized she didn't have anything to say back because Monica was right. She *was* pitiful. They were both pitiful. How the hell had all this happened, anyway?

"I don't have to listen to this."

She strode toward the door, regretting the day she'd ever offered to help Monica get a job when she was clearly a horrible, conniving woman who'd stop at nothing to get what she wanted. To think she'd felt sorry for her.

You're too nice, Susan told herself. *Nice, nice, nice. And it gets you into trouble every time.*

She left the bar and headed toward home, clutching the steering wheel so tightly her fingers hurt, anger and humiliation oozing out of every pore. Well, now Monica knew how she felt about Paul, so that meant everybody at the hospital would probably know. And if it ever got back to him...

Oh, God. How embarrassing would that be?

Even the most boring gossip tended to sweep through the hospital like a tropical storm, so she knew this little tidbit would be upgraded to hurricane status in no time. She pictured ducking around corners every time Paul approached so she wouldn't have to look him in the eye.

She fumed all the way home, then pulled into her driveway and went inside. Lani sat in the dining room, typing away on the computer.

"Lani," she said sharply. "Are you on the Internet?"

"I needed to print something for a class assignment." She hit a button and the printer groaned to life.

"You're only supposed to be on it when I'm home."

"So was I supposed to wait around all night to finish my homework?"

Don't fight with her. It'll only make a bad night worse.

A minute later Lani pulled the sheet out of the printer, looked it over, then grabbed a textbook from her backpack.

"Oh," she said, pulling out another piece of paper. "Here's something for you."

Susan took it from her, and when she read it a primal scream rose in the back of her throat.

Linda Markham? Snacks for the basketball team?

"Tomorrow?" Susan said. "She wants these *tomorrow*?" Then she looked at the date the note was sent. "Lani? How long have you had this?"

"I don't know. A couple of days."

"You can't bury this stuff in your backpack! Not if it's something I have to do!"

"I forgot."

"I don't believe this," Susan said, still reading. "She wants me to make granola bars. Why not *buy* granola bars?"

"The other moms make stuff."

Susan yanked open the pantry door. "The other moms make stuff because Linda Markham browbeats them into it. What is *with* that woman, anyway? Here. A package of Oreos. That'll do."

Lani looked horrified. "I can't take those!"

"Why not?"

"Because it's for basketball. It has to be healthy!"

"Please. Like your teammates never eat cookies?"

"All the other kids bring homemade stuff. If I took those, do you know how stupid I'd feel?"

Susan closed her eyes, gritting her teeth. If kids had a choice between Oreo cookies and granola bars, she was pretty sure which one they'd pick. So why couldn't she just send something the girls would actually like?

Then she thought about Lani standing there with a package of Oreos while the other kids were showing

up with dried apricots from a home dehydrator and
baked bagel chips rubbed with fresh garlic. She'd feel
silly and stupid in an angsty teen environment where
kids already felt silly and stupid without any help from
a mother with no time to bake.

Susan had a choice. She could tell Linda Markham
to go to hell, or she could drive to the store, get the
ingredients and stay up for another hour making
granola bars so her child wouldn't be a horrible outcast.

With a heavy sigh, she grabbed her purse and
headed for the door. As she drove, she found herself
thinking back to everything that had happened that
day, and her eyes filled with tears again. She blinked
and clenched the steering wheel harder, wishing the
earth would open up and swallow Linda Markham.
With luck, Monica would get caught up in the vortex
and go right down with her.

For the next week, Susan managed to avoid Monica
at work, hoping the whole time that she'd keep what
had happened between them to herself. When a few
days passed and nobody came up to Susan and said, *so,
I hear you have a thing for Paul White*, she relaxed a little.
Even Evie seemed unaware that anything was going
on, and she was the most amazing gossip processor
Susan had ever seen. She sucked in every detail, re-
arranged it until it sounded as salacious as possible,
then broadcast it again with the wicked efficiency of

a deranged new anchor on prime-time TV. If she wasn't talking about it, Susan knew Monica hadn't said a word to anyone.

Of course, that didn't mean she wasn't going after Paul every spare moment she had.

On Monday night, Susan arrived at class with only a minute to spare, but this time she'd planned it that way so she wouldn't have to talk to Monica. She was already there when Susan slid into her seat, and she made a point of looking away and saying nothing.

"Hey, girls," Tonya said. "Have you kissed and made up yet?"

When neither of them said anything, Tonya sighed heavily. "Guess not."

Out of the corner of her eye, Susan saw Monica redouble her arrogant expression, as if she was just a little too good for the rest of the people present and most certainly better than Susan. It seemed to Susan that she'd worked extra hard at looking stylish and attractive tonight, probably to rub in what was already obvious: if it came down to a head-to-head battle between them for a particular man, Susan wouldn't have a prayer of winning.

Danforth came to attention. "Is there a problem between you two ladies?"

"Nothing we need to get into here," Susan said.

"On the contrary. If you're angry with each other, this is precisely the place to get into it."

"I'll pass," Monica said.

"Me, too," Susan said.

"If you'll allow me to guide the discussion, we can resolve this issue without resorting to pugilism."

Tonya screwed up her face. "What the hell is pugilism?"

Danforth closed his eyes for a moment. "Fighting."

"Well, then why don't you just say fighting?"

Susan thought that was a really excellent point, but Danforth merely let out a long-suffering sigh, as if he was wondering what he'd done so wrong as to end up in the company of morons. He turned to her and Monica.

"What is the nature of your disagreement?"

Monica shook her head. "I really don't think this is an appropriate topic for discussion. Susan will only get defensive again."

Susan whipped around. "I'm *not* defensive."

"Oh, boy," Tonya said. "Here it comes."

"On second thought, maybe we *should* get into it," Susan said. "I mean, the other night Monica actually seemed proud of the fact that she sleeps with men to get jobs."

Monica glared at her. "At least I've still got it. Use it or lose it, Susan."

"If I choose to use it, it won't be to seduce a man into helping me get a job!"

"If you choose to use it, I'll drop dead with shock!"

"When I *use it* is absolutely no business of yours!"

"Likewise. Which is why I intend to go after Paul whether you like it or—"

"Stop!"

At the sound of Tonya's voice, Monica's and Susan's mouths fell shut. Tonya turned to Danforth.

"Okay," she said. "Here's the deal. Monica targeted a man at work to seduce, thinking she can get a better job if he puts in a good word for her. Only the guy happens to be somebody Susan has the hots for. But since Susan doesn't have the guts to go after him herself, Monica figures he's fair game. Basically, they both want to get into his pants but for entirely different reasons."

Danforth stared at Tonya dumbly for a moment, then slowly removed his glasses and rubbed his eyes. "All right, ladies. Let's back up a bit. Ms. Roth, perhaps you could give Ms. Saltzman an I-Message to tell her how you feel."

Dammit. Susan did *not* want to do this.

"Ms. Roth?"

"Oh, all right." She took a deep breath. "I feel angry when you talk about seducing Paul to get ahead at work."

"Because?" Danforth said.

Susan paused. "Because it's the wrong thing to do."

Monica rolled her eyes. "What a cop-out."

"It's *not* a cop-out! It's wrong to seduce him when you have no real interest in him other than getting ahead!"

"Okay, Susan. Here's my I-Message. *I* don't get why you won't just admit you like the guy!"

"You stated that in an improper format," Danforth said. "Perhaps you'd like to—"

"Will you hold on a minute?" Monica held up her palm to Danforth, then turned to Susan. "What are you so afraid of?"

"Afraid? I'm not afraid of anything."

"Then why won't you admit how you feel about Paul?"

Susan faced Monica, hating the way she looked so pristine and perfect when Susan felt anything but. "Okay, Monica. You're right. I do have a thing for him. But I don't stand a chance against you. So go ahead. Seduce him. Will that make you happy?"

Susan turned away, staring down at her desktop. Danforth focused on Monica. "She asked you a question."

"What?" Monica said.

"She asked if it would make you happy."

More seconds ticked by. Finally Monica sighed, then turned to Susan. "No. It wouldn't make me happy. Not if it made you miserable."

Susan nodded, still staring at her desktop.

"Excellent, ladies," Danforth said. "As you can see, it's not as difficult as you think to resolve—"

"Wait," Monica said. "I'm not through yet." She turned to Susan. "Let's see. I-Message." She took a deep breath. "I feel frustrated when you say you want more out of life, but you're too insecure to go after it."

"Because?" Danforth said.

"I'm not insecure," Susan said. She turned away, fuming a little. "I'm not. I'm just..." She shook her head in resignation. "Okay. So I'm insecure."

"You're divorced," Monica said. "That means you're free to date other men. What's stopping you?"

Susan shrugged weakly. "I told you before, I have so much going on. When would I have the time to date? And when it comes right down to it, do I really need one more thing in my life to keep up with?" She shook her head. "It would only make things more crazy than they already—"

"Oh, will you knock it off?" Monica said.

"What?"

Monica turned to Danforth. "That's not the issue. She's just too scared to step out there, so she's coming up with every excuse in the book why she can't. Well, I'm sorry, but I'm not buying any of it."

"Is that true, Ms. Roth?" Danforth said. "Is it fear that keeps you from pursing more opportunities in your life?"

She wanted desperately to deny that. But she couldn't. Monica was so right that Susan wanted to scream or cry or pound the desktop—anything to let out the frustration she felt. She wanted to be that woman that some man couldn't take his eyes off of. She wanted it so badly that sometimes she couldn't think about anything else. But someone like Monica, who had been wrapping men around her finger since she was old enough to talk, couldn't possibly understand that it wasn't as simple as she made it out to be.

"I have to go to the bathroom."

Susan got up, grabbed her purse and left the room, sure she was going to cry if she didn't. She went into the ladies' room and sat down on the sofa, folding her arms and gritting her teeth, feeling like the biggest loser alive.

A minute later, the bathroom door opened and Monica and Tonya came in. Susan closed her eyes. She did *not* want to deal with this.

"Will you guys go away?" Susan said. "I'll be back there in a minute."

Instead, they came and sat down on either side of her, boxing her in and making her feel as if she was on the hot seat all over again.

"Look," Monica said. "I didn't mean to upset you. It's just that you complain about how you haven't had a date since your divorce, yet you don't do anything to make it happen."

"Oh, yeah? What am I supposed to do?"

"Well, you might start by doing something to make yourself attractive to a man."

"Hey, you try being a divorced mother. See how much time you have for making yourself beautiful."

"It doesn't take any more time to get the right haircut than it does the wrong one."

"Thanks, Monica. I appreciate that."

Monica rolled her eyes. "All I'm saying is that just because you're a mother and a working woman, it doesn't mean you can't look fabulous."

Susan couldn't remember a time when she'd ever looked fabulous. She usually looked nice. Reasonably attractive, sometimes. But that was about all she'd ever been able to accomplish.

"Men are shallow," Tonya said. "They won't look past the surface, at least at first. That's why you have to doll it up a little bit."

"Okay," Susan said. "Here's the truth. I met Don on a blind date, and I think both of us just took the path of least resistance. Before that, I barely dated at all. I'm just not very good at it, especially after all this time."

"That doesn't mean you can't get back in the game," Monica said.

Susan sighed. "No. You were right. Look at me. I can shop all day long, but if I don't know what to buy what good does it do me? I can get my hair cut, but if I don't know what looks good how am I supposed to tell them what to do?"

Monica turned to Tonya. "Well, I've got the shopping covered."

Tonya smiled. "And I can do her hair."

"Now, wait a minute, you guys—"

"And I throw great parties," Monica said.

Susan felt a stab of foreboding. "Party?"

"We'll invite everyone at the hospital. The fun people, anyway. And I'll make absolutely certain that Paul is there."

"No," Susan said, shaking her head. "No party. I'm not good at parties."

"You don't have to be good at parties. All you have to do is stand there looking beautiful. Let Paul see another side to Nurse Susan. We'll do it this Saturday night."

"That soon?" Susan said, already feeling the anxiety. "Don't you need time to plan?"

"Nope. There's nothing to throwing a party. Believe me, people will be all over it. Nobody wants to give one, but everybody wants to come to one. I can have invitations e-mailed by tomorrow at noon. But first I'll make sure Paul will be there."

Susan thought she was going to be sick. She'd been known to bring heart attack victims back from the dead. That was no big deal. But the very idea of dressing up, going to a party and hoping to talk to a man she was attracted to positively scared her to death.

"So you're not going to try to seduce him?" Susan asked Monica.

Monica rolled her eyes. "No, I'm not going to try to seduce him. He's all yours. Assuming you actually get out there and *do* something about it."

Susan sighed. "I don't know if I can."

"Yes or no. Do you want your ex-husband to be the only one with a love life?"

Susan thought about Don and Marla and San Francisco and wedding bells. Then she thought about sitting home at night watching sitcom reruns with a bowl of popcorn in her lap. Unless she did something differently, in a few years she'd still be watching those reruns, only her dentures would keep her from eating the popcorn.

"No," she said. "I don't."

"Well, then," Monica said with a smile. "As of right now, Operation New Susan is officially underway."

CHAPTER 9

Early the next Saturday afternoon, Monica took Susan on a clothes shopping expedition, and Susan felt uptight the entire time. She hated department stores. They felt like undulating tides of clothes and shoes and handbags and jewelry, veritable seas of fashion she had no idea how to navigate. Monica, on the other hand, had no problem swimming right through it.

Susan made an attempt to browse through a few racks, only to have Monica take her by the wrist, pull her into a dressing room and tell her to stay put. A few minutes later, she brought in an armload of clothes. Susan tried on several things, rolled her eyes and sent them right back out again, telling Monica she was forty-five, not twenty-five.

But the worst part was the remarkably efficient three-way mirror in the dressing room, set at just the right angle that a woman could see 360 degrees of herself. Susan was standing there between try-ons, wearing only a pair of panties and a bra, when she happened to glance over her shoulder and caught the first good look at her own butt that she'd had in years. She remembered that part of her anatomy as round and maybe even a little perky. What she saw were two mounds of flesh, flat as the plains of west Texas, drooping halfway to her knees. Like a dog chasing its tail, she spun one way, then the other, hoping the view would change. No such luck.

That experience alone had almost sent her screaming from the dressing room, but Monica talked her down off the ledge, then convinced her to buy a few outfits that were trendy without making her feel like a complete fool. Susan bought a pair of low-rise pants, which felt weird, but the tunic top that went with them didn't look half-bad. She bought a few knit tops in the too-bright colors Monica insisted on, but at least the styles were nice. And finally she agreed to one of those short little sweater-jackets, telling Monica she didn't mind as long as she didn't insist on the one with fur around the collar. Monica made her buy jewelry, too, bigger pieces than she was used to wearing. *You have to make a statement*, Monica kept saying, but Susan didn't want that statement to be *Look at that poor old woman trying to look like a teenager*.

For the party, Monica talked her into buying a casual dress that looked more like a nightgown, but it was a pretty shade of teal-blue without lace, ruffles or flounces. And heels. They were only two inches, but they felt positively stratospheric when Susan hadn't worn a pair in years. But she had to admit that once she was out of her work clothes and put those heels on with that dress, her legs didn't look all that bad. She left the store feeling pretty upbeat, as if transforming herself on the outside was going to help her make the changes she wanted on the inside.

Then they headed to Tonya's shop, a small store-front on Montoya Avenue with a sign in the window that advertised a discount on acrylic nails and another one that said walk-ins were welcome. Tonya had closed the shop early this afternoon so she could devote her full time and attention to giving Susan a new do. But as soon as they sat down with the hair style books, Susan felt uptight all over again.

"No. No way. I can't do that with my hair. No." She slapped the book shut. "I need something more conservative."

"Conservative has kept you a very boring person," Tonya said. "And hair is no big deal, anyway. If it's too long, cut off more. If it's too short, wait a few months and it'll grow out again. But there's no doubt about it. You gotta go blond."

"No way. I'd look dumb as a blonde. They'd laugh me right out of the PTA."

"Will you stop being such a *mother*? Men don't make passes at PTA presidents."

"It's just not me."

"Exactly."

"I just don't think—"

Tonya spun Susan around, put a hand on either armrest of her chair and stared down at her. "Picture Don. Picture his fiancée. Picture the wild sex they're having. Now picture yourself at home, popping Hershey's Kisses and doing the *TV Guide* crossword puzzle."

Susan felt sick at the thought of that, or maybe it was just the corn dog she'd had at the mall. No...wait. It was definitely envy. Envy in a very ugly shade of green.

"I hear you. Do something, even if it's a little weird. But blond is still out."

"Okay, then. How about just a few shades lighter? And highlights. It'll brighten up your complexion and cover the gray. You don't have much, but it's there. No sense reminding a man of his mother right off the bat." Tonya stood back up and turned Susan around to face the mirror again. "Trust me, sweetie. You're going to look amazing."

An hour later, Susan sat staring at herself in the mirror, trying to reconcile her new hair with her old face. Sticking it in a ponytail was going to be out from now on, but she had to admit she liked it shorter. It made her feel younger. Less momlike. She kept touching it, unable to believe it was actually on her head.

"So you really like it?" Tonya said.

"Yeah. I think I do."

"It does look fabulous," Monica said. "Paul is going to die when he sees you."

"Don't get carried away," Susan said. "It's still me under here." She sighed. "I have no idea what to say to him."

"Don't worry. I'll help you out."

"Please don't make it obvious, Monica. *Please*."

"Sweetie, I'm an expert at these things. Trust me."

Susan heard bells chime against glass. She turned to see a man coming into the shop. And there was only one thing she could say about him.

Wow.

He was tall and broad-shouldered, dressed in jeans, boots and a flannel shirt, carrying a small toolbox. He had dark hair, dark eyes and the kind of classically handsome face that would make just about any woman do a double take. Susan had never seen one of those soft-core porn flicks before, but she was pretty sure if they were casting the part of a sexy handyman who shows up to make a repressed house-wife's dreams come true, this guy could have walked right into the role.

"Dale?" Tonya said. "What are you doing here?"

This was Tonya's husband? Susan's mouth fell open a little, and she noticed Monica's did, too. Somehow this just didn't compute. It wasn't that Tonya was un-attractive, but this was a man who could probably have just about any woman he wanted on his looks alone.

Instead he was married to a good ol' Texas girl with the fashion sense of a hooker and the personality of a bulldozer.

"I saw Crystal at the bank yesterday," Dale said. "She told me something's wrong with one of the dryers. I thought…you know. I'd come by and take a look at it."

Tonya shrugged. "Sure, honey. Beats having to pay a repairman."

Her words were nonchalant, but her posture had suddenly gone rigid, and Susan could tell there was more going on in Tonya's mind than getting her dryer fixed.

"I didn't know you were open today," Dale said.

"I'm not. Susan and Monica are friends of mine. We were doing Susan's hair, and—"

"I can come back another time."

"No need for that."

"Is it running but not heating? Or not running at all?"

"Running but not heating."

"Okay. I'll take a look at it."

Dale headed for the back room. As he passed by, Monica's admiring gaze went from his shoulders to his waist and landed squarely on his ass.

"He's your husband?" Monica said, as Dale disappeared into the other room.

"Yes," Tonya said.

"I hope you don't mind if I go back there and watch him strap on a tool belt."

"Monica!" Susan said. "The last thing Tonya needs is another woman looking at her husband."

Tonya grabbed a can of hairspray. "Look all you want to," she said, giving Susan's hair a quick squirt. "You think I care?"

Susan took the hairspray from Tonya and set it down on the counter. "Yeah, I think you care."

"I told you, I don't."

She picked up a broom and started sweeping up the hair on the floor.

"Tonya," Susan said, "do you really think he came here to fix that dryer?"

"Why else would he be here?"

"He clearly came to talk to you. Do you want to talk to him?"

Tonya shrugged. "I don't know. Maybe if he'll say he's sorry, I *might* think about forgiving him."

"I don't know," Monica said, shaking her head. "If a man cheats once, chances are he'll do it again."

"I'm well aware of that," Tonya said. "I have a cheating ex-husband to prove it. And a cheating father. And two cheating stepfathers. I know all about the behavior of cheating men."

Susan was stunned. Tonya had experienced all that and now this? No wonder it was tearing her up so much.

"Maybe this thing with Dale was just an isolated incident," Susan said. "If you love him, it might be worth giving it another try. Just forgive him for what he's done and go from there."

"Assuming he wants to be forgiven."

"Try him and see."

Tonya put the broom up against the wall and squared her shoulders. "Okay. Sure. I'll go talk to him. Can't hurt, I suppose. But nothing's gonna get fixed between us until I get that apology and he swears he'll never do it again."

Her words were full of bravado, but Susan could tell by Tonya's hesitance as she walked toward the back room just how shook up she was. She'd been hurt in the past. Badly. And Susan couldn't even imagine how it must feel to have one more man she loved do it to her all over again.

Tonya felt as jittery as a june bug as she walked to the back room, her mind all fuzzy as she tried to think about what she was going to say. She stood quietly at the door for a moment, looking at Dale on his knees with the dryer pulled out. Even though they'd been married for three years, sometimes their relationship still felt brand-new, and she swore she could spend hours just staring at him and be perfectly happy. He had the faint shadow of a beard on his cheeks and chin, which made her think about how it felt to lie beneath him, her cheek pressed against his, feeling so rough and scratchy but so warm and masculine that she never cared at all.

"Hey," she said finally.

He looked around. "Hey."

He removed the last screw, pulled the back off the dryer and set it along the wall.

"So what do you suppose is the matter with it?" Tonya asked.

"It's probably the coil. If so, I'll run out and get a new one."

He turned back to the dryer and started to check it out, only to hesitate for a moment, then toss his screwdriver to the ground. He slowly came to his feet.

"Tonya?"

"Yeah?"

"Do you think maybe we could talk for a minute?"

Her heart skipped with hope. "What do you want to talk about?"

He took a few steps toward her. "I don't want to fight with you anymore. I'm so tired of fighting."

Oh, thank God. "Actually," she said, "I'm getting a little tired of it myself."

Dale let out a breath. "It's been hell without you. I can't sleep at night, I get all distracted at work—"

"I know. Me, too."

The air seemed to quiver between them, suddenly filled with hope for the future. He inched forward, lifting his hand as if to touch her, then dropping it back to his side, as if he wasn't sure how she'd react if he did. Five seconds passed, then ten, as they stood there staring at each other.

Tonya thought about what Susan had said. *If you love him, it might be worth giving it another try.* And she did love him. No matter what had happened between them, no matter how dumb and deluded it made her feel, she still loved him.

"So where do we go from here?" Dale asked.

Tonya moved a little closer to him. "Maybe we could…I don't know. Do you suppose we could just put this behind us and move on?"

Dale nodded. "That's all I've ever wanted."

"Good," Tonya said on a breath. "That's good. Just tell me what happened, and then we can forget all about it."

Dale froze. "What did you say?"

"Just tell me what happened, and say you won't do it again. That's all I want."

"Tonya—"

She held up her palm. "No. I know how I've been in the past, but I won't hold it against you. I won't throw it in your face the next time we have an argument. I swear I won't do that. But if you keep denying it—"

"I'm denying it because it never happened!"

"You can't deny what people saw, Dale," she said, trying to be patient. "But it's okay. I forgive you for it. I swear I do. I just want you to admit it, and then we'll never talk about it again."

"No. I have no intention of—"

"Just say it!"

Dale clamped his teeth together and glared at her. "Get this straight, Tonya. I'm never going to admit to something I didn't do. *Never.*"

He grabbed the screwdriver from the floor, stuffed it into the toolbox and slammed it shut. He snatched it up and started out of the room.

"Fine!" Tonya shouted, following him. "Leave! I don't care!"

"Good thing, because I'm out of here."

Dale strode through the front of the shop, yanked open the door and stormed out. Tonya watched through the plate glass as he slammed the toolbox into the back of his pickup. As he drove away, dead silence fell over the shop.

"I suppose you heard all that," Tonya said.

Another long silence.

"Tonya?" Susan said.

"What?"

"Is it possible he's telling you the truth?"

"If that were possible, we wouldn't be having this problem."

"But he's still denying it. How can that be if you know for sure—"

"Hey, when another woman is hanging all over him at a bar, and then he leaves with her and they go to her house, it doesn't take a genius to fill in the blanks."

"Wait a minute," Susan said. "That's your evidence?"

Both Tonya and Monica turned to Susan with pointed stares.

"Okay," Susan said. "I admit it looks bad. But what's Dale's story?"

"He said he took her home because she was too drunk to drive. Like I haven't heard that one before?"

"Sounds reasonable to me."

"Listen carefully, Susan. When Crystal, one of my stylists, saw Dale leave with that woman, she called me right away. I got in my car and parked down the block from the woman's house. A few minutes later, Dale pulled up and they went inside. I saw *that* with my own eyes."

"How long was he in the house?"

"Almost forty-five minutes."

"And what was his explanation for that?"

"He said the woman was really sick. Throwing up. He said he didn't feel like he ought to leave her."

"Sounds like a pretty good explanation to me."

"Hey, I know the woman he was with. Kendra Willis can have her hand down a man's pants so fast it'd make your head spin, drunk or not. If he was in there with her, *something* happened."

"Did you ask her about it?" Monica asked.

"She said she was too drunk to remember anything but being in her bedroom with him," Tonya said. "But I think she was scared to admit what happened because she was afraid of a few flying dishes herself."

"So what are you going to do now?" Susan asked.

Tonya paused, suddenly feeling very tired. "I don't know."

"Do you love him?" Susan said.

Tonya wished that one tiny word didn't have such a big impact. She felt so mixed up, every emotion in the book lumped together inside her. She felt angry. Impatient. Frustrated. But most of all, she was scared that she and Dale were nearing the point on the road where there was no going back no matter what the truth was.

"Love's not the issue," Tonya said. "I didn't hesitate to cut loose the last husband who cheated on me."

"Seems to me you're hesitating now," Susan said. "Why is that?"

"I don't want to talk about this anymore."

She grabbed the broom and started sweeping again. When she glanced up at Susan and Monica, she didn't like the way they were looking back at her. Even Monica was staring at her as if she pitied her, and Monica didn't seem like the kind of person who pitied anyone.

Tonya gritted her teeth, blinking back tears, hating herself for loving a man so much who was clearly going to lie to her forever.

CHAPTER 10

At six-thirty that evening, Susan pulled up in front of Monica's condo, feeling like a different person in the dress and heels and with a new haircut. But different was good, wasn't it? If she wanted something different in her life, she had to *do* something different. But all this meant that eventually she was going to have to talk to Paul, and just the thought of that made her palms sweat.

She arrived half an hour early so she could help Monica with the food. Her condo wasn't big, but it was beautifully decorated, which meant her taste extended past fashion right into home decorating. The first thing Monica did, though, was give Susan a critical once-over. Everything below the neck seemed to pass muster. Then Monica looked at her face and frowned.

"Okay. This isn't going to cut it."

"What?" Susan asked.

"Come with me."

Monica led her to her bathroom, hauled out her makeup, and for the next ten minutes she swiped and brushed and blended, then turned Susan around to let her see how she looked.

She stared at herself in the mirror, dumbfounded. "You're kidding, right?"

"It's perfect," Monica said.

"Yeah, if I'm planning on walking the streets."

"The light is going to be dim tonight. That means your makeup needs to be heavier."

"Or maybe I could be a televangelist."

"You're just not used to it."

"Is the circus taking clown applications?"

"Will you *stop*? You look fabulous."

Susan wasn't buying that. Not for one moment.

But when seven o'clock came and the doorbell started ringing, the women were surprised to see the new Susan, giving her lots of oohs and ahhs over her new haircut and her new dress. And for once the men actually seemed to see her rather than look right through her.

Or maybe that was just wishful thinking.

She sipped a glass of wine as she waited for Paul to arrive. Usually she drank red, but Monica had poured her a glass of white. *If you spill it*, she said, *it won't show*. Good advice. Whenever she got nervous, her hands shook. God only knew where this wine was going to end up when she saw Paul walk through the door.

Monica, on the other hand, was so relaxed that

Susan felt envious. Born to be a hostess, she flowed through the room effortlessly, greeting people at the door and making them feel right at home. Before long, her modest-sized condo was bursting at the seams. She'd already told Susan that the best parties were crowded ones where people drank a lot and were forced to stand really close to one other. If that was true, this was going to be the social event of the season.

Then Evie showed up. She had on a pair of pilled polyester pants, a green sweatshirt and the same ugly, disagreeable face she always wore. She caught sight of Susan and gave her a once-over, looking as if she'd smelled something rotten.

"What did you do to yourself?" she asked.

"What do you mean?"

"The whole hair and dress and heels thing. Why didn't somebody tell me this was a costume party?"

"Somebody clearly did," said Carl, who had walked up behind her. "You came as a bitch." He leaned in and gave Susan a peck on the cheek. "Don't listen to her. You look fabulous."

Evie rolled her eyes and headed for the dining room. If past holiday buffets at work were any indication, she was going to Hooverize half the food before anyone else had a chance to pick up a plate.

"Explain to me why she was invited?" Carl said.

"Monica was afraid if she didn't invite her, she'd slash her tires."

"Ah."

"Snubbing Evie is something one does at one's peril."

"So what prompted the sudden makeover?" Carl asked.

"It was Monica's idea."

"Listen to her. She clearly knows what she's talking about."

"So is that your new boyfriend?" Susan asked, nodding toward a guy getting two glasses of wine from Monica. He was an attractive Hispanic man with dark shoulder length hair and a pierced eyebrow.

"Yes. That's Emilio. What do you think?"

"Hmm. Very nice. When does he graduate from high school?"

Carl drew back. "I'll have you know this one is twenty-four years old."

Susan smiled. "He still plays video games, doesn't he?"

"Yes," Carl said dreamily. "There's just something about a young man and his joystick that does it for me every time." He patted her shoulder. "I'll talk to you later."

As he walked off, Susan turned back to keep watch on the front door. People kept showing up, but Paul didn't. Monica said he'd been enthusiastic when he'd responded to her invitation, but Susan was beginning to wonder if something had come up or he'd just decided not to come after all. She took another sip of wine, trying to hit that target area between drinking enough to loosen up and being so bombed she couldn't stand up.

Another knock. Monica swept over to the door and opened it, and Paul stepped inside. Susan felt relieved. Self-conscious. A tiny bit drunk. And apprehensive, because now that he was here, it meant she had to follow through with her role in the plan.

He handed Monica a bottle of wine, then she took his coat. Susan didn't think she'd ever seen him when he wasn't wearing a tie, but tonight he wore a pair of casual slacks and a lightweight sweater that fit his tall, lean body exactly right. He wasn't exactly the kind of handsome that turned every woman's head, but it wasn't just his looks that had turned Susan's. She loved the sound of his voice, and the way he greeted everyone in the hospital by name and the little crinkles around his eyes that said he smiled a lot. He was the kind of man you could sit with in front of a fire on a cold night and feel as if everything was right with the world.

Monica furtively shifted her gaze to Susan. *Don't just stand there. Get over here.* So she wove through a few people until she reached the front door, trying for a nice, natural smile that ended up feeling totally unnatural.

Deep breath. Just do it.

"Hi, Paul."

He turned. Froze. Blinked. Tilted his head and narrowed his eyes.

"Susan?"

Monica leaned toward Paul and said in a teasing voice, "Of course it's Susan, silly. You haven't been drinking already, have you?"

"Uh, no." He turned back to Susan. "You just look…different."

Oh, God. Different always equaled awful. *Always.*

"Of course she looks different," Monica said, with a light little laugh and a wave of her hand. "You didn't expect her to show up in those hideous scrubs and sneakers they make the nurses wear, did you?"

"Uh…no. Of course not."

His dumbfounded gaze was still glued to Susan, telling her he hated the way she looked. Hated it. And he was right. At her age, she had no business having this hairstyle, this hair color, this makeup, this dress. She was a middle-aged mother without a sexy bone in her body, and it was time to quit trying to be something she wasn't.

But just as she was wishing she could vanish into thin air, the most wondrous thing happened.

He smiled.

Susan blinked with surprise. Looked over her shoulder. Nope. Nobody was there.

He was smiling at her.

"I think," he said, that smile growing broader still, "that we need to get away from the hospital more often."

For a minute Susan didn't know what he meant, but then it all came together and suddenly she felt as if the clouds had parted and sunlight was streaming down from heaven.

"Paul?" Monica said. "What can I get you to drink? Wine? Beer?"

"Beer's fine," he said, his gaze still on Susan.

Monica gave Susan a wink and a knowing look that said, *My work here is done* and headed toward the kitchen. And then they were standing there alone, and Susan couldn't think of a single thing to say.

"It was nice of Monica to have this party," Paul said. "She's very social, isn't she?"

He didn't know the half of it. "Yes. She is."

"Lots of people showed up."

"Uh-huh."

More silence. Susan's face heated up, and she prayed her cheeks weren't turning red. Maybe she could blame it on the alcohol. *Say something*, she told herself. *Anything*.

But still she stood there, mute as a giraffe and feeling just about as conspicuous.

But somehow, they started to talk. First about work, which she expected, and then Paul turned and looked at Monica's bookshelves. He asked Susan if she was a reader, and she said she was, even though it had been at least six months since she'd read anything besides cereal boxes and patient charts. They walked over to the bookshelves and checked out the titles. Monica had already told Susan that she got books from a used book store just to make the shelf look pretty, but when Paul commented on her eclectic taste Susan simply agreed. Right about then, she'd have agreed with him if he'd told her the moon was made of cheese.

Monica brought Paul a beer, and by the time he'd drained half of it, Susan had finished her wine. The alcohol buzzed in her head in a very pleasant way, drowning out the chatter in the room until all she heard was Paul. Everything he said seemed interesting or funny or both, and every time she laughed her earrings bobbed back and forth, reminding her that, for once, she looked soft and feminine and maybe just a little bit pretty. She was going to thank Monica profusely for making her buy them.

Talking about books segued into a discussion about movies they'd both seen recently. When they agreed that they liked romantic comedies but hated historical dramas, Susan realized they had more in common than she'd ever imagined. Or at least it felt that way when he was talking to her and smiling at her and probably lying about the romantic comedy thing, but she didn't care. At the very least, they'd probably never get into any arguments in the new releases aisle at Blockbuster.

"You really do look great tonight," Paul said. "Sorry I acted so surprised earlier."

"It's okay. It's hard to imagine what a person might look like when they're not walking the halls of Baptist Memorial Hospital."

"From now on," he said with a smile, "I'll remember."

Susan hoped it wasn't the alcohol that was making her hear that tone in his voice, the one that went beyond his usual nice and into the realm of interested. But she was just so incredibly bad at reading the signs that she simply couldn't trust herself.

"Why, Paul!" Susan heard a woman's voice say. "I had no idea you were going to be here!"

Susan turned to see Cecily Bradford, pretty blond Cecily who worked in admissions, smiling at Paul. When he turned and smiled back at her, suddenly Susan felt old and frumpy again.

"I've been meaning to drop by your office and talk to you," Cecily said, flashing her ultrawhite porcelain-veneer smile. "I have some questions about my retirement account I know only you can answer."

Of course, that led Paul to ask her what questions she had because he was too nice not to. *Damn it.* The woman had thirty years to go until retirement. Couldn't her questions wait at least until Monday?

"Hey, Susan!"

Susan turned to see Carl motioning to her from across the room. *Oh, God.* What did he want?

She turned to excuse herself from Paul, but he was looking at Cecily—what man wouldn't?—and

Susan's heart sank. So she just slipped away and went over to Carl, who wanted her to tell Emilio the story of how she'd once had a woman in the E.R. who denied being pregnant, then gave birth to twins. Why that was so hilarious to him, she didn't know, except that he'd had enough to drink by that time that just about anything was funny.

Once she looked back around to where Paul had been standing, he was gone. After a quick glance around the room, she spotted him on the sofa. Cecily was with him, sitting so close to him their thighs touched, and Susan felt a streak of jealousy. She wanted to be the one touching his thigh. Or maybe he'd rather be touching Cecily, and the thought made Susan want to spill an entire glass of red wine right down the front of the woman's too-tight blouse.

Monica came up beside her. "What's Paul doing sitting with Cecily? You were holding the fort just fine. Then she moved in to attack, and you just handed her the keys."

"Carl wanted me to—"

"Forget Carl. It's not Carl you're after. It's Paul. Keep your eyes on the prize. Cecily has been locked on to him since he arrived."

"She has?"

"Of course she has."

"How do you *know* these things?"

"It's no different than watching animal mating

habits on The Discovery Channel. She's been fluffing her feathers for some time now, which means you need to do a little fluffing of your own."

"Things were going pretty well until she showed up. Paul and I were having a really nice conversation. We like the same books. The same movies and all kinds of other things."

"Yes. He's definitely interested."

"Do you really think so?"

"Of course. I could tell the moment he laid eyes on you."

"Well, I couldn't. I swore he hated the way I look."

"Nope. When a man is speechless like that, it means he's thinking with another part of his anatomy besides his brain. That's a good thing. But men have short attention spans. They can be like kids at Halloween. One piece of candy looks really good until they see what's at the next house." Monica peered into the living room. "Here's what we'll do. I'll get Cecily to move, and then you sit down next to Paul."

"How are you going to do that?"

"You leave that to me. Once Cecily's out of the picture, I want you to ask him out."

"*What?*"

"Just think of a movie that's playing in town that he might not have seen, and tell him it might be fun to go together. No specific time or day. Just hit him a ball and see if he hits it back."

"But if he says no—"

"He's not going to say no to, 'It might be fun to go to a movie together sometime.'"

Susan closed her eyes. "This is making me sick."

"You'll be fine. Just go back out there with me. Casually wander over to the sofa. I'll get Cecily up, and you sit down."

They went back to the living room, where the party noise had hit a whole new decibel level. Cecily was still on the sofa with Paul, only now she'd turned her body so that he couldn't help but stare right down the front of her shirt. Since she had way more to stare at than Susan did, insecurity hit her hard all over again.

Still, she did as Monica told her and took up a position beside the arm of the sofa. Monica moved around strategically and, after a few minutes, caught Cecily's eye. She put her finger to her cheek and got really expressive with her eyes as if trying to tell Cecily she had ketchup on her face or parsley in her teeth. Cecily's hand went to her own face, her eyes widening with distress. Monica made a few "come here" motions with her fingertips, and Cecily immediately got up and followed her into the other room.

Susan turned back to the sofa. *It's now or never. Do it!*

She circled past the arm of the sofa and sat down in the space that Cecily had vacated. Paul turned around, saw her sitting there and gave her a smile.

"I was just getting up," he told her.

She drooped with disappointment.

"To find you. But it looks as if you've found me."

When his smile grew broader still, Susan almost melted with joy.

"I don't think we finished our conversation," he said.

"No," she replied. "We didn't, did we?"

As they started to talk again, the party seemed to grow louder still, to the point where they had to lean in every time they spoke to each other to be heard. As they drew closer, Susan could smell a few faint notes of the cologne he wore, a woodsy scent that fit him perfectly.

Was there anything about this man she didn't like?

After a while, she glanced across the room to see Cecily eyeing her and Paul, and Susan swore she could see the woman's calculating little brain working, even at that distance. But when Cecily moved in to sit in a chair adjacent to the sofa, Paul didn't even acknowledge her. He just kept talking to Susan. To her astonishment, she was the one he *wanted* sitting next to him, even though Cecily was younger and blonder and cuter. The thought of that made Susan glow from the inside out.

She had no idea how long they sat there, but soon she became aware that people were leaving. She glanced at her watch. It was after ten. She blinked, then looked again. How in the world could that much time have passed?

Finally they rose from the sofa and made their way to the front door. Monica handed them their coats and said goodbye, giving Susan a furtive thumbs-up when Paul's back was turned, and mouthed, *Call me*.

Paul walked Susan to her car. The night air was cold, but it felt good after the warmth of Monica's condo.

"Good party," Paul said.

"It was, wasn't it?"

"I gotta tell you, though. The thought of coming here tonight made me a little uptight. It's funny how you can get out of the swing of things, and suddenly you realize it's been forever since you socialized with anyone. I was afraid I'd forgotten how."

"Me, too," Susan agreed. "So why did you decide to come?"

He shrugged. "It was just time to get out again. As much as I may feel like it sometimes, I'm not over the hill yet. How about you? Why did you come?"

Because Monica had the party just for you and me. I couldn't very well not show up.

"It was just time for me, too," she said.

"So it looks as if we're in the same boat."

She smiled. "Yeah. It looks that way."

They stared at each other a long time. Suddenly Susan was aware of everything about him: the faint indentations in his cheeks that became dimples when he smiled. The way his sandy brown hair seemed to take on a golden tint in the dim light of the streetlamp overhead. The smile that said he genuinely liked being with her. And that gave her the courage to form the words in her mind that Monica had told her to say.

Unfortunately, she couldn't get them to come out her mouth.

"Well," Paul said finally, when the silence dragged out too long. "I guess I'd better go."

"Me, too."

"I'll see you at work on Monday."

"Yeah," she said. "Have a safe drive home."

Paul wished her the same, then turned around to walk to his car. Suddenly the words Monica was sure to berate her with started banging around inside her head.

Susan! What do you mean you let him get away without asking him out? Are you crazy?

"Paul?"

He turned back, looking at her expectantly. "Yes?"

"I was just wondering...we both like movies, so I thought it might be fun to go to one sometime. You know. Together."

Paul blinked with surprise. "Are you asking me out?"

He looked so shocked that Susan knew it had been the wrong thing to say. She shouldn't even have opened her mouth. What could she do now but tell the truth?

"Uh...yeah. I guess I was."

He heaved a big sigh of relief. "Thank God."

"What?"

He walked back to where she stood by her car. "You just saved me from having to work up the nerve to ask *you* out."

Susan felt a rush of relief herself. "Really?"

"Yeah. I've been thinking about it all night. But I'd talked myself out of it. Told myself I could do it Monday. And if not Monday, then there was always Tuesday. I was afraid I was going to go through the whole week like that. I'm just glad you're not as uptight as I am."

"Oh, yeah? Not uptight? Check this out." She held up her hands. They were shaking. "You'd think I have a neurological disorder or something."

He caught her hands and held them for a moment. "They're not shaking now."

Susan swallowed hard. "No. They're not."

He held them a little longer, then slowly released them, but not before it registered in Susan's mind just how good it felt to have a man touch her again.

"This is a little embarrassing to admit," Paul said, "but I've been divorced for two years, and I haven't been on a date since then. That's why I'm a little rusty."

Susan couldn't help laughing. When she saw his look of distress, she put her hand on his arm and shook her head. "I'm sorry. I'm not laughing at you. It's just that you're telling the story of my life. I've been divorced a year and a half, and I haven't dated, either."

When he smiled again, it dissolved any lingering doubt she felt about jumping back into the dating world again.

"My ex-husband has my daughter on the weekends," she said. "How about next Saturday night?"

Paul winced. "Wouldn't you know it? I'm tied up then. I'm leaving town Saturday morning and I won't be back until the following Saturday. It's a family thing. I'm sorry."

"Oh."

"Could we go some night next week?"

"Actually, I'm not too sure how my daughter's going to react to me dating. She just found out her father is getting married again, and she's not taking it very well."

"So she doesn't like the idea of Mom and Dad having separate lives?"

"Exactly."

"How about the Saturday I get back, then? Two weeks from tonight. Would that work?"

Susan smiled. "It's a date."

"Okay, then. Dinner and a movie. Can we talk about the specifics on Monday?"

"Yeah. That'd be fine."

"It was fun tonight. I'm really glad I came."

"Me, too."

Still smiling, he slowly backed away from her car, then turned around and walked to his. When Susan got into her car, her hands were shaking all over again.

You did it, she thought. *You actually did it.*

She felt giddy all the way home, and when she got there she called Monica to tell her what had happened. They chattered like a couple of teenagers for a good twenty minutes. Even though it was nearly eleven-thirty by the time she hung up the phone, Susan was still so wired she didn't doze off until nearly one o'clock, when sheer exhaustion was the only thing that finally took enough of the edge off her excitement to let her fall sleep.

CHAPTER 11

By the time Don brought Lani home on Sunday evening, Susan still felt as if she were walking on air. She'd had so much energy that she'd straightened out the pantry, vacuumed and dusted the whole house, cleaned both bathrooms and did three loads of laundry. Now she was cooking dinner, flitting around the kitchen like Tinkerbell on speed. And it felt *good*.

Lani came through the front door and walked into the kitchen. She dumped her stuff onto the table, then stopped short and stared at Susan.

"What did you do to your hair?"

All at once Susan realized that Lani hadn't seen her since Monica and Tonya's makeover.

"I got it cut before the party last night," Susan said. "And added color and highlights."

"Why did you do that?"

"I don't know," Susan said with a smile, passing her fingers through her hair. "I just felt like a change. Oh! Come here. I want to show you something."

She turned down the burner on the stove, then led

Lani to her bedroom closet, where she pulled out the clothes Monica had insisted she buy.

"These are *yours?*" Lani said.

"Of course they're mine." She grabbed the blue dress and held it up in front of her. "I wore this to the party. What do you think?"

Lani made a face. "I don't like it. And your hair's all wrong, too."

Susan blinked with surprise, feeling a little hurt. "Why do you say that?"

"It's like you're trying to look like me, or something. Kaylee's mother does that. It looks dumb."

"Come on, Lani. I'm not trying to look like you. I'm just trying to update my wardrobe a little. What's wrong with that?"

"I'm just telling you what I think. You always tell me what you think about my hair and clothes."

"The last time you changed your hair, you turned it blue."

"That was just Kool-Aid," she said. "It washed out. You changed yours for good."

Determined that Lani wasn't going to ruin her good mood, Susan hummed her way over to the closet and hung the clothes back up again.

"So you went to a party last night?" Lani said.

"Yeah, and I had a really good time."

When she came out of the closet, Lani gave her hair

the once-over again, suspicion slowly spreading across her face. "Were there guys there?"

"Of course there were. I work with a lot of men." She closed the closet door. "I spent a lot of time talking to Paul White. He's the director of human resources at the hospital."

She couldn't even say his name without smiling. But the longer she smiled, the more Lani frowned.

"You like him, don't you?" Lani asked.

Susan felt a twinge of apprehension. "Of course I like him," she said as offhandedly as she could. "He's a nice man."

To Susan's surprise, Lani's face started to crumple and tears filled her eyes. "I don't want a stepfather."

Susan drew back with surprise. "What are you talking about?"

"Everybody I know hates their stepfathers."

"Who says you're getting a stepfather?"

"You said you liked the guy."

"Lani. Liking a guy and marrying him are worlds apart."

"So are you going out with him?"

Oh, God. Why had she even mentioned Paul's name? Why?

Because she'd never expected Lani to make the leap from her mother talking to a man to her mother *marrying* that man.

"No," Susan said. "Not right now." Which she told

herself wasn't exactly a lie. They were going out two weeks from right now.

Lani plopped down on Susan's bed, her arms crossed, her jaw tight with anger. "Why does everything have to change? You don't even look like my mom anymore."

"I haven't changed at all," she told Lani. "It's still me, even with new hair and clothes."

"But that's just what Dad did. He started dressing all different, and he bought that car, and suddenly he wasn't Dad anymore. Then Marla came along. I hate her."

"I don't think you really hate her."

"Will you stop telling me how I feel?" she shouted. "I know how I feel! I already lost Dad. I don't want to lose you, too!"

Lani leaped up off Susan's bed and stomped out of the room. She went into her bedroom and slammed the door behind her. A moment later, her stereo came on. Very loudly.

Susan tried to stay calm. Rationally, she knew a lot of this was just teenage angst out of control. Lani had never been one to keep her emotions bottled up. Still, junior high had been hard enough for her without her parents splitting up, and Susan had always carried around a heaping dose of divorce guilt over that.

She left her bedroom and started down the hall to talk to Lani, just as she always did after a blow-up, wondering what in the world she could say to clean up this particular mess.

Then her strides shortened. She stopped. For at least a minute, she stood in the hall, thinking about that.

And she decided she wasn't going to do it.

This time she wasn't going to give in to Lani's hysterics. She wasn't going to wait around to start dating again until everyone else in her life said it was okay because there was little chance of that ever happening. What Lani didn't know wouldn't hurt her, anyway. Susan was an adult, after all, and her daughter didn't need to know everything about her life. The Saturdays Lani was with Don were Susan's time to do what she pleased, and being with Paul pleased her very much.

For once she was entitled to a little bit of happiness, and nobody was going to take it away from her.

The following evening, Tonya came into the classroom and found Susan and Monica already there. It was five till seven and Danforth hadn't arrived, so she settled into a chair to get the scoop from Susan.

"So, tell me what happened at the party. I've been dying to know. Was it good?"

She told Tonya everything that had happened. Then she added that they'd also had lunch together in the cafeteria today, and they'd talked so much she barely ate anything.

"A great guy and weight loss, too," Tonya said. "That does sound perfect."

Tonya truly was happy for Susan. She was looking different, acting different. Tonya wished her life was going as well.

Just then, Danforth arrived and took his seat. "Hello, ladies. I trust everyone had a calm, noncon-frontational week?"

Sure, Tonya thought. *Calm and nonconfrontational. Unless you count that horrible fight I had with my husband when he came to my shop.*

Danforth stroked his chin, gazing across the room, as if waiting for God to give him the words to speak.

"Tonight we're going to be talking about cognitive distortion. For the purposes of anger management, this comes in the form of negative thought processes. Such thought processes aren't based in reality, but they can feel very real to the person experiencing them, thus triggering anger. Once you learn to recognize their onset, you can learn to control them and thus control your anger. We'll be dealing with three of them tonight."

Tonya yawned, not even bothering to try to disguise it. One of these days, Danforth might actually figure out just how boring he was.

"Number one," Danforth went on, "is jumping to conclusions. Assuming something to be negative which may not be negative at all. Number two is mental filtering. This is focusing exclusively on the negative aspect of a situation, while ignoring any positive features. And number three is emotional reasoning. Drawing conclusions based on how you feel rather than on objective reality, often colored by prior experience which may not be applicable to the current problem."

He took a few sheets of paper from his briefcase and handed one to each of them.

"On this sheet are the three negative thought processes. I want you to list at least one way in the past that you've succumbed to each one."

Tonya looked it over for a few minutes. In general, she was a pretty positive person, so nothing was coming to her right off the bat. Monica and Susan were writing stuff, though, so she figured she should, too. If only she could think of something to write.

"Is there a problem, Ms. Rutherford?" Danforth asked.

"Sorry. I'm having a hard time thinking of anything."

Susan shot a glance her way.

"What?" Tonya asked.

"Nothing."

A minute later, Susan pushed her form aside and crossed her arms. Okay, so she was finished. Tonya chewed on the end of her pen, still trying to think.

"Still blocked?" Danforth said.

"Yep. Drawing a blank."

"Oh, come *on*," Susan said under her breath.

"Is there something you want to say?" Tonya asked her.

Susan stared at her a long time. "Just think for a minute. Where right now in your life might you be jumping to a conclusion?"

Tonya knew immediately what Susan was talking about. "I told you before. I don't want to discuss that."

"Ladies?" Danforth said. "Do we have some discord?"

"Nope," Tonya said. "None at all."

"Yes, we do," Susan said. "She has no real proof her husband cheated on her."

"That's not true," Tonya said.

"And how about this mental filtering thing?" Susan went on. "You're ignoring the good parts of your marriage and focusing only on this one incident."

"Yeah? Well, it's a pretty damned big incident."

"And emotional reasoning. 'Drawing conclusions based on how you feel rather than on objective reality, often colored by prior experience which may not be applicable to the current problem.' Tonya...that's *you*."

"I *don't* want to talk about this!"

Susan sighed. "Look, I can see why you'd be a little emotional about the issue. If I'd had all those cheating men in my life, I would be, too. But it doesn't mean Dale is one of them."

"Ms. Rutherford?" Danforth said. "Am I to understand that you didn't actually witness your husband's infidelity?"

Tonya folded her arms, glaring at him. "No. Not

exactly. But I've been through this before. I know the signs."

"The signs?"

"My first husband cheated. My father cheated. My stepfathers cheated. *Men cheat.*"

Danforth had the nerve to chuckle at that. "Are you telling me it's your belief that because of the infidelity of a few individuals, it means that half the population is unfaithful?"

"From what I've seen in my life, it's hard *not* to jump to that conclusion."

"I don't know your specific circumstances. Your husband may well be guilty. But after years as a psychologist and witnessing all manner of infidelity, my best recommendation to you is that you respond as rationally and reasonably as possible. And that means you should give him the benefit of any doubt."

"What?"

"If one is going to err, Ms. Rutherford, it's always better to do it in a positive direction rather than a negative one. That way, your conscience will always be clear." He turned to Monica. "Now, Ms. Saltzman? Would you share what you've written with the class, please?"

Tonya stayed so mad through the rest of the class that she didn't even hear anything Monica or Susan said. Benefit of the doubt? Danforth was just saying that because he was a man, and all men stuck together.

And it wasn't her conscience that was the issue here. It was Dale's.

When class was over, she headed straight out the door and into the parking lot, the cold night air hitting her like a slap in the face.

"Tonya! Wait!"

She heard Susan's voice behind her, but she kept on walking toward her car. Susan and Monica caught up with her just as she was opening the door.

"Tonya!"

Tonya spun around, facing Susan head-on. "I expect Danforth to be an ass. To give me a hard time. But I don't expect it from you."

"The other day at your shop," Susan said, "I could see how miserable you were. I can tell how much you love Dale. Don't let what's happened to you in the past cause you to make a mistake now."

Tonya knew Susan was just trying to get her to be optimistic. But she just didn't know what to think anymore. Her mind was so muddled she couldn't make sense out of anything. She leaned against her car with a heavy breath, the quiet of the night settling the air between them.

"You just don't know what it's like being married to Dale," Tonya said. "You should see the way other women look at him sometimes."

"Sweetie, he's a gorgeous man," Monica said. "I couldn't name you a woman who *wouldn't* look at him."

"Exactly! Am I supposed to just ignore that?"

"Come on, Tonya," Susan said. "Just because they look at him doesn't mean they're out to steal him away from you."

Steal him away from you.

Susan had no idea how words like those tripped something inside her that made her feel sick right to her bones.

"How long have you and Dale been married?" Monica said.

"Three years."

"Was he married before?"

"Yes. For eleven years."

"Why did he get a divorce?"

"He didn't." A gust of cold air whipped across them, and Tonya pulled her coat more closely around her. "His wife died of cancer."

Nobody talked for a while. The mention of death had a way of doing that to a conversation. But that left Tonya to think about that one thing she always tried to keep out of her mind: Dale's dead wife. Tonya had always had the terrible feeling that a person found true love only once in a lifetime, and Dale had already found his.

"Dale and I are so different in so many ways," Tonya said. "I come from a family so screwed up we'd make Dr. Phil throw in the towel. But Dale's got this really big family where everyone stays married forever. It took me a long time to get used to going to family gatherings where people didn't yell at each other. It's just so perfect. And I'm not."

"Come on, Tonya," Susan said. "He married you for a reason, didn't he?"

"Yeah, but to tell you the truth, I've never been too sure exactly what it was. I'm nothing like his other wife was. The way he describes her, she was really sweet and quiet and all. And I think he really loved her, you know?"

"I'm sure he loves you, too," Susan said.

God, she hoped so. With all her heart. Because if he didn't, they wouldn't have a chance of working this out. She just wished that no matter how guilty Dale looked, she could wake up tomorrow morning and believe he was telling the truth. That all her doubts about him loving her forever would disappear. But the way things were now, she was always going to wonder if someday in the future she'd see that lipstick on his shirt, or find that receipt in his pocket, or pick up the phone to hear the other woman on the other end and realize what a fool she'd been.

The following Friday, it was nearly eleven o'clock before Susan was able to stop for a breather. It had been unusually busy in the E.R. that morning, which was a good thing because it kept her mind off the slow crawl of time from the beginning of her shift until noon, when she could finally go to lunch.

Every day this week, she'd gotten up half an hour

early to make herself look as nice as she possibly could. She put on makeup, and because she was getting pretty good with a round brush and a blow dryer, her hair looked almost as nice as it had when Tonya did it. She couldn't do much about the ugly clothes she wore to work, but at least she was in a place where a lot of people were forced to dress ugly together and it wasn't just her alone committing a fashion faux pas.

Then, at noon every day, she'd gone to the cafeteria to meet Paul for lunch. Since she could count the number of times she'd seen him there before this week on one hand, she had to conclude that he was there for the company and not for the food.

She liked the way he laughed. The way he listened. The way he said nothing sometimes but just looked at her. During those times, she could tell he was thinking the same thoughts she was, thoughts that were full of promise for the future.

A little wiped out by all the activity that morning, Susan headed to the soda machine in the alcove outside the admissions office to get a shot of caffeine. For the first time in her adult life, she felt disappointed that it was almost the weekend. Paul would be leaving town tomorrow morning, and he wouldn't be back for a week. On Saturday night, though, they'd have a wonderful date making up for lost time.

Susan plugged quarters into the machine, pushed the button for a Diet Coke and a can clattered out.

"Change of plans."

Susan grabbed the can and turned around to find Paul standing behind her. Just looking at him made hot little shivers shoot between her shoulders.

"No cafeteria today," he said.

"You don't want to meet for lunch?"

He pulled a business card from his pocket and gave it to her. She saw a residential address he'd written on the back.

"It's less than five minutes away. And it has something the cafeteria doesn't."

"What's that?"

"You and me," he said quietly. "And nobody else."

For a moment, she couldn't breathe, her heart suddenly going wild. His house. He wanted her to come to his house.

"I'll stop somewhere and grab something for us to eat," he said. "Twelve o'clock?"

She tucked the card into her pocket, her gaze never leaving his. "Twelve o'clock."

He gave her a faint smile and a nod to seal the deal, then walked away. Susan leaned against the soda machine, still clutching the can, her eyes closing in sheer delight as she thought about spending time alone with a man she was crazy about.

An hour later, Susan pulled up in front of Paul's house, and her jaw dropped. He couldn't live here. No *way* could he live here. She had to double-check the address, then check it again before she finally accepted that she really had arrived at his house and not the state penitentiary.

It sat at the head of a cul-de-sac, a two-story gray structure that looked like four or five gigantic boxes stacked on top of one another, covered in stucco that was sanded smooth. A second-floor balcony had a metal pipe railing, which was almost as cold as the tinted plate glass windows. Boxwood shrubs grew with military precision, as if any leaf that fell out of formation would be whacked off instantly. The only thing that made any sense at all was the For Sale sign in the front yard.

She got out of the car, went to the door and knocked. A few moments later, Paul answered. Standing there with his hand on the doorknob and a smile on his face, he looked as warm and comfortable as ever, even against a backdrop of industrial carpet, white walls and weird modern art in tones of gray, gray and more gray. The furnishings were equally bleak. She looked around dumbly.

"Sorry," Paul said. "I should have warned you."

She came inside and he shut the door. "It's…uh…"

"Cold? Stark? Barren?"

"It's not exactly…you."

"You're right. It's my ex-wife. She moved to Chicago, and I got the house in the divorce."

She gazed around, thinking of telling him that it really wasn't all that bad, but it was, and she'd never been a very good liar. "At least you're selling it."

"It's been on the market for a year and a half. Exactly two people have made it through the door to see the inside. With luck, a tornado will level it so I can collect on the insurance."

"There's always arson."

"Nope. It has to be an act of God. I'd never be able to convince anyone that I didn't deliberately burn this place to the ground." He motioned toward another room. "Come on. You haven't lived until you've seen the kitchen."

Susan followed him into the kitchen, where she saw a gray tile floor, granite countertops, gray cabinets and more plate glass. With the harsh fluorescent lighting, the place looked like a futuristic torture chamber.

"Have you considered getting a few plants?" Susan asked. "Might brighten the place up a little."

"I had one once. It lived a week. I think it committed suicide."

"I'm having a hard time picturing you married to a woman who appreciated this."

"We were together for twenty-four years," Paul said. "But we only spent two years here in Leavenworth. When our daughters were still at home, we lived in a normal house. Then my wife wanted this place. Said it was her dream home."

"I can't believe she talked you into it."

"Actually, our marriage was pretty shaky by the time we moved here. She talked a lot about wanting her own identity. I really didn't get that at the time, but she was obviously unhappy, and since she really wanted this house I went along with it. Thought it might help things."

"So this was the identity she was after?"

"I finally realized what she wanted was to live in a house that was totally different from the one where she'd been a mother to two kids. Only it turned out that we'd already passed the point where anything would make her happy."

"So when did you realize divorce was coming?"

"Hard to say, really. We'd been drifting apart for a long time, but we were both so busy that we really didn't see it. Then, once the girls were out of the house and all the noise was gone, the silence was pretty deafening. And believe me, when we moved in here and added that silence to a house that was already pretty cold, it really did feel like solitary confinement." He opened up one of the take-out containers. "*Moo goo gai pan* work for you? I didn't want to get anything too spicy until I knew what you liked."

"Sounds great. I'll eat just about anything."

He pulled out a container of rice. "So what's your story?"

She shrugged. "Don and I were just two people

who should never have been married in the first place. We were totally incompatible. But since we both came from families that avoid confrontation, it took us a while to end it."

"Hmm," he said, "I notice you didn't mind confronting a certain coffeehouse geek."

Susan felt a shot of embarrassment. "I can't believe I did that. I was lucky Andi didn't fire me."

"Oh, we discussed the issue. With the police involved, we had to. But since we both knew you, and we'd both been to the coffeehouse and experienced that guy, we decided just to look the other way."

"I still shouldn't have done it."

"I'm glad you did. It's what told me that there might be more to you than I thought."

"What? A bad temper?"

"No. To tell you the truth, I liked that you stood up for yourself."

"Even if it got me arrested?"

He flashed her a smile. "Even if it got you arrested."

He kept looking at her with those warm green eyes and that engaging smile, holding her gaze a second or two beyond the way mere friends would look at each other, just as he'd been doing for the past several days when they'd eaten lunch in the cafeteria.

"In that cabinet behind you," he said finally. "Could you get a couple of plates?"

Tearing her gaze away, she turned around and

grabbed two stoneware plates. He pulled out a spoon to dish the food, then glanced into the sack again.

"Damn. They did it again."

"What?"

"Forgot to put in the soy sauce. But I think I have some." He handed Susan the spoon, then headed for the fridge. "I actually thought about cooking something for us," he said, digging around in the fridge, "but trust me. It really is better this way."

"I don't care what we eat. I didn't come here for the food."

For a moment, Paul's searching stopped, and silence filled the kitchen. She glanced over her shoulder to see him standing by the open door, meeting her eyes in one of those too-long stares that signaled something else going on. Suddenly she realized what she'd said, and what his eyes were saying: *If you didn't come for the food, what did you come for?*

A little shaky, she turned back to the counter, digging the spoon into the rice, feeling hot all over. She thought maybe she should say something, such as, *I'm here because you're such an excellent conversationalist* or *because I heard you lived in a mausoleum and I had to see it for myself.*

But the truth was that she didn't give a damn about food, conversation or this god-awful house, and Paul knew it.

The refrigerator door *swooshed* shut. She heard his

footsteps behind her. Too nervous to turn around, she just stood there, holding the rice-filled spoon in midair. His footsteps stopped, leaving him standing so close behind her she could feel the heat radiating from his body even in this ridiculously cold house.

Then he put his hand against her shoulder.

It was as if somebody had fired up a defibrillator to 360 joules and zapped her with it. She couldn't breathe. She couldn't move. She just stood there, weak-kneed, as he edged his hand down her arm to her elbow, then slid it toward her hand. He pulled the spoon away from her and set it back into the container, then eased his other hand around her waist. With a single fingertip, he teased her hair behind her ear, leaned in and kissed her neck.

Swallowing hard, she slowly turned around and stared up at him. She must have had a funny look on her face because a look of distress came over his.

"Oh, God," he said. "I think I read that wrong."

Susan still couldn't speak.

"I told you it's been a while," he said sheepishly. "I'm sorry. I really didn't mean—" He closed his eyes for a moment, then turned away. "Let's just have lunch, okay?"

He slid one of the take-out containers toward him. She grabbed his wrist. She held it for a moment, then slowly met his eyes.

"You didn't read anything wrong," she said.

She took a step toward him, her eyes never leaving

his. Her hand still on his wrist, she eased up next to him and kissed him.

For a moment he just let it happen. Then all at once he took her in his arms and kissed her back, and every bit of the desire that had been building up inside her since the night of the party came pouring out. She'd been starving for this for so long now, trying to tell herself she wasn't, until he had shown up at Monica's party and the hunger pangs had become so excruciating she couldn't ignore them any longer. And judging from what Paul was doing, he felt exactly the same way, giving her one long, hot kiss after another, eventually making her so dizzy she could barely stand.

When her knees buckled a little, he backed off for a moment, breathing hard, and she knew he was checking her reaction because things were moving so fast. She responded by diving toward him again, wanting more, and he seemed more than happy to give it to her. He backed her against the counter and trapped her there, pressing his body against hers and kissing her some more, one hand tucked behind her neck, the other sliding down her hip to her thigh and back up again. When he moved his hand beneath her shirt and stroked her back, skin on skin, his touch growing progressively more urgent, she couldn't mistake where this was going. She felt as if she were in one of those scenes from a movie where the hero and heroine just can't get enough of each other, and all Susan could think was *more. I want more.*

Then suddenly Paul pulled away, holding her at arm's length.

"What?" she said.

"Is this going where I think it's going?"

"I think it is."

"Maybe we'd better slow down."

"Do you want to slow down?"

He stared at her, breathing hard. "It's been a long time, Susan. I'm not exactly thinking straight right now. The last thing I want to do is push you into something you don't want."

But she did want it. She was normally so mature and sensible that she was dying for something impulsive and impetuous. She thought about Don and how he'd moved on with his life, and she was ready to do a little moving on herself. Yes, it was crazy. But a dose of crazy was exactly what she needed right now.

She took hold of his tie. She slid it out of its knot and slowly, slowly pulled it from around his neck in a sensual sweep of silk against cotton, her eyes never leaving his. He turned his gaze down and watched it hit the floor, then looked back at Susan.

"I have another room I want to show you," he said.

"And I'd love to see it."

He took her by the hand and led her down the hall, walking so fast she had to hurry to keep up. The house passed by in a monochromatic blur. Her heart. God, her *heart*. Tachycardia had never felt so good.

Wait. Horrible thought. What underwear did she have on? There was that pair with the hole at the waistband. What if she was actually wearing those? How embarrassing would that be?

No, wait. She'd seen those in the laundry basket last night.

Throw those damned things out when you get home.

Okay. Her underwear was intact. Utilitarian, but intact. Forget about wearing nice underwear in case she was in an accident. From now on, she was going to wear nice underwear in case she had hot, spur-of-the-moment, lunch-hour sex.

Seconds later they reached a room that should have been warm and sensual but was just as frigid as the rest of the house. Only a cold, cold woman could have decorated a bedroom like this, and Susan imagined icicles hanging off his ex's nose.

"Sorry," he said, taking her in his arms again, "I wish I had something better to offer than a jail cell."

"I'll just pretend it's a conjugal visit."

He laughed at that, and she felt a rush of pure pleasure, because she didn't remember a time in her life when she'd laughed during sex. *It's not a laughing matter* had been Don's unspoken motto, and sooner or later that had become the law of the land in a country already famous for its lack of levity.

Paul kissed her again, and at the same time he

wrapped one hand around her waist and moved the other one up to cradle her breast. He fanned his thumb across her nipple, once, twice, a dozen times, until a tiny moan rose in the back of her throat, and she thought, *Thank God. I'm going to make it past age forty-five with my privates intact.*

"I didn't plan this," he murmured in her ear. "I swear I didn't. I just thought we'd have a nice lunch together. Then you said what you did, and it made me think of this. It was a leap, I know. But considering where my mind has been lately…"

He kissed her mouth again, his hands moving over her body in a way that made her skin prickle and her flesh rise up in little goose bumps.

"It's a little late to be asking," Susan said, "but are you sure we can do this?"

"Do what?"

"Uh…fraternize."

"The hospital has no rule against it. I'm director of human resources. I know these things."

He circled his arms around her as he kissed her again, his hands roaming impatiently down her back to skim the lower curve of her ass. Grasping it snugly, he pulled her body tightly against his as he kissed her, which should have felt good considering the part of him that was now pressing against the right part of her, but suddenly all she could think about was that damned dressing room mirror and the way her butt had looked in it.

No, don't touch me there. Anywhere but there.

As if he'd read her mind, he brought his hands back up, this time slipping them beneath her shirt and flattening his palms against her lower back. *Yes. That's better.* Still kissing her, he moved his hands up, bringing her shirt up with them. Then suddenly it wasn't better at all, because Susan realized that in just a minute he was going to be doing something worse than touching her ass and every other part of her.

He was going to be *seeing* it.

She pulled away suddenly, her eyes blinking involuntarily, and gazed around the room. Where had all this damned *daylight* come from?

"Paul?"

"Yes?" he said, drawing her close again, his breath hot against her neck.

"I'm forty-five years old, you know."

He kissed her earlobe. "Yeah. I know."

"I've had a baby."

"Uh-huh."

"Gravity and I aren't exactly on speaking terms."

He slid his hands under her shirt again, searching for the hook of her bra. Thank God it was in the front.

"Wait," she said.

"What?"

"I was thinking maybe we could postpone this."

He looked a little panicked. "Postpone it?"

"Like, until it's dark out? On a moonless night?"

He looked at her blankly for a moment. Then his face broke into a smile. "So you're forty-five. I'm forty-eight, which means I've had three more years of gravitational pull than you have."

"Men wear age better."

"Don't bet on that.

"Susan," he said, "we're in this together, okay? Neither of us is twenty-five anymore."

We're in this together. How fast could she fall in love with a man before the cynics would say it was impossible?

"Are we okay?" he asked.

She smiled. "You've been warned."

"And it was totally unnecessary."

As he leaned in for another kiss, her self-consciousness faded away, leaving her so very glad to be with a man who knew just what to say to a woman with a sudden body image crisis. Now, *that* was a turn-on. She could only imagine what his answer would be to the eternal question, *Do these pants make me look fat?* Whatever it was, she'd probably have an orgasm on the spot.

Before she knew it, her shirt was over her head and on the floor, providing some much-needed color to the ugly gray carpet. She unbuttoned Paul's shirt in record time and he took it off, but as he was reaching for her again, he stopped short, a panicked expression rising on his face.

"Uh-oh."

"What?"

"Uh…we may have a problem."

"What?"

His eyes got progressively wider. "I don't suppose…"

"*What?*"

"You don't happen to carry any condoms with you, do you?"

It took a second for Susan to grasp the full scope of what that question meant, and when she did it was her turn to panic. "Are you telling me you don't have—"

"Stay there," he said, pointing at her as he hurried to the bathroom. "Don't move!"

Susan heard drawers and cabinet doors opening and closing. Intermittent cussing. More banging around. Finally he walked out, slumped against the door frame and looked at her dumbly. "And to think I was a Boy Scout."

She wilted with disappointment. "Nothing?"

"Unless you think a Ziploc bag will do the trick."

For several seconds they just stood there staring at each other, Paul shirtless, Susan in her pants and a bra, feeling the aftershocks of a "coitus interruptus" that was one for the record books.

"If you needed any more proof that I really didn't plan this," Paul said, "there you go." He shook his head. "Am I smooth, or what?"

They stood there a while longer, just staring at each other in disbelief. Then Susan began to realize the absurdity of the situation and started to smile. Paul smiled back. Then the laughter began—at first, just light little chuckles at the nooner that wasn't, but before long they escalated into something that could only be called hysteria, echoing off the cold gray walls until the monochromatic room seemed to bloom into Technicolor. They stumbled to the middle of the room and fell into each other's arms.

"What a mess," Paul said, still laughing.

"It's because we're old, isn't it?" Susan said. "Young people these days always carry condoms."

"Well, you can bet from now on that I'm stocking every room in the house." He brushed her hair away from her forehead and kissed her there. "Think we can try this again? Say, a week from tomorrow?"

"Oh, yeah."

He sighed. "I wish I weren't leaving in the morning."

Susan didn't like the sound of that, either, but maybe it would be a good thing after all. It would give her the opportunity to go shopping for some decent undergarments. Pick out a nice perfume. Make sure she was shaved and lotioned and powdered so everything would be perfect.

She smiled. "The time will go fast."

"Not fast enough," he said, and when he kissed her again she had the feeling he was right. The next seven days just might end up being the longest week of her life.

CHAPTER 12

When the comb-over guy walked into Tonya's shop for his monthly cut, she thought about passing him off to one of the other stylists, but Elsie was doing a perm and Crystal was taking a late lunch. Tonya had just finished with a customer and had an empty chair, which meant she had to deal with him. Cutting a man's hair an inch long on one side and six inches long on the other, then sweeping it over and gluing it to his head offended every sensibility she had. What kind of man seriously believed his head looked better with ugly hair than no hair at all?

She thought about what Danforth had said, which really hadn't helped at all, and came to the conclusion that she was stuck. Like it or not, this guy was going to continue to be a walking billboard for her shop, which meant she might as well put a big sign up in her window that read We Give Horrific Haircuts.

As always, she cut it the way he wanted it even though it looked like hell. The longer she looked at that horrible cut, the more she thought about Dale. He had nice, thick hair that felt so good to run her fingers through, and every time she cut it she wanted to make love to him right then and there. It had gotten to where she couldn't turn around anymore without something reminding her of him.

Especially the sirens.

Every time she heard one, she imagined him going out on a call and worried about him even more than usual. Dale took too many chances sometimes, like the time he went back into a burning building for an old lady's dog because she was crying so hard about losing him. But Dale was like that. Always doing something for somebody, on the job or off.

As she finished ringing up the comb-over guy, Crystal came back from lunch, still sucking on the straw of a soda cup. She passed him, smirking a little behind his back as she watched him walk to his car.

She went to her station and set down her cup. "Did I ever tell you about the time I went waterskiing with a guy who had a comb-over? Now, *that* was hilarious."

"You're late getting back from lunch," Tonya said.

"I don't have a customer until two o'clock."

"We might get walk-ins."

"Yeah, we get a lot of those early on Monday afternoon."

Tonya grabbed the cape and gave it a shake. "You never know who's coming in. I want you here on time."

"Tonya, for God's sake. I'm five minutes late."

"Hey," Tonya said sharply. "Just be here when you're supposed to be, okay?"

Crystal eyed her carefully. "What's the matter with you?"

Tonya drew back. "Just because I think you should get back from lunch on time something's the *matter* with me?"

Crystal glanced to the back of the shop, where Elsie was rinsing her customer's hair, then turned to stare hard at Tonya, dropping her voice. "Tonya, look. You've been really bitchy and short-tempered lately and not just with me and the other girls. You've been that way with customers sometimes, too, you know. You need to fix this thing with Dale."

"Dale has nothing to do with anything."

"Oh, will you cut out the crap? Dale has everything to do with everything where you're concerned."

Crystal was right. She was so right that Tonya wanted to tear out her own hair.

"Just how am I supposed to fix things?" Tonya asked. "Should I just go home and pretend nothing ever happened?"

"I don't know," Crystal said. "Maybe you should."

"Yeah? Aren't you the one who was so quick to call me that night when you saw him leaving the bar with Kendra? Now you think we should just kiss and make up?"

Crystal stared at Tonya a moment, as if she was undecided about something. "Maybe I shouldn't tell you this, but…"

Tonya came to attention. "What?"

"I saw Dale having lunch today at Sparky's. He was with somebody."

Tonya felt a shiver of apprehension. *Please don't tell me it was another woman, or I'm going to turn that dead dryer into scrap metal with my bare hands.*

"Who?" she said, barely able to croak out the word.

"Larry," Crystal said.

His cousin. Thank God. Tonya breathed a huge sigh of relief. "Yeah, they get together every once in a while."

Crystal nodded, but Tonya felt that funny little quiver in the air, as if there was still something else.

"What?" Tonya said.

"Isn't Larry…"

"What?"

"A divorce lawyer?"

Tonya froze. He was. That had never meant anything before, but now…

"What are you trying to say, Crystal? That they were discussing *business?*"

"Hey, I'm not saying anything."

"Dale and Larry meet for lunch a lot. It means *nothing.*"

"You're probably right." Crystal twirled a strand of her hair around her finger. "Of course, it's been almost a month since all this came down. And you haven't seen him since you had that fight."

"Will you cut it out? I don't need you speculating on my relationship with Dale."

"I'm just trying to help."

"Help? You call that help? Next you're going to be taking bets with the other girls on when we're going to break up for good."

For the rest of the afternoon, Tonya couldn't get Dale's lunch with Larry out of her mind. She'd told Crystal it didn't mean a thing, but she was afraid it did. Maybe Dale really did want a divorce.

But wasn't that what she should want, too? Dale had cheated, just like her first husband, which meant she should be cutting him loose and forgetting all about him.

So why wasn't she?

She didn't know. This whole thing had left her so damned confused because what was in her head was clashing so hard with what was in her heart. She wanted Dale back so much, but maybe that was only because she was still so heartbroken that he'd cheated on her. Maybe she'd get up one morning and realize she was still trying to hang on to something she ought to be letting go of for good.

Or maybe Dale was going to make that decision for both of them by heading to divorce court.

She couldn't imagine how things could ever be right

between them again. The only thing she knew for sure was that if he wanted a divorce, any chance they had of making their marriage work was going to be gone.

One way or another, she had to find out what he was up to.

"Tonight we're going to talk about some ways to control your anger," Danforth said, as he kicked off class number six. "I suggest a three-pronged approach. Expressing, suppressing and calming."

Monica sighed heavily, thinking that if only she had something three-pronged and really sharp she could do away with Danforth altogether. And she was quite certain that Tonya and Susan would help her dispose of the body.

"Expressing your feelings in an assertive but not aggressive manner is the healthiest way to articulate your anger. This means being respectful of others as you make clear what your needs are."

That was the biggest bunch of nonsense Monica had ever heard. How was she supposed to be respectful of a man who screwed her out of a job by screwing another woman into it?

As Danforth droned on, Monica realized she had figured out what the deal was with these anger management classes. If you did something violent, they sent you to listen to Danforth for eight weeks, and you swore to be as sweet as a little lamb for the rest of your life out of fear of ending up here again.

"For instance, Ms. Saltzman. Isn't it possible that if only you had discussed the situation with your boss, you could have come to some kind of understanding rather than resorting to violence?"

Oh, God. Why did he always have to pick on one of them? "That's not likely."

"Even so, you accomplished nothing by assaulting the man. Had you the self-control to suppress your anger, you never would have been arrested."

"I don't know," Monica said, injecting her voice with a sarcastic lilt. "I've always heard that suppressing anger is unhealthy. It leads to high blood pressure, heart problems—"

"And letting out anger in inappropriate ways leads to court proceedings and jail sentences," Danforth said. "There are situations in which one should suppress one's anger and then find a way to redirect it."

As much as she was giving Danforth a hard time, in her heart she was beginning to believe he was right. If only she'd kept her cool with Jerry, at least she'd probably still have some kind of job at the bank, one where she didn't have to sleep with the boss. She would have emerged with a little bit of dignity. Then she could have stood by and watched Nora O'Dell lose hers.

"The secret," Danforth said, "is to transfer the

energy your anger creates into behavior that is productive and nonviolent."

He pushed his glasses up his too-big nose and went on about anger suppression and redirection and then talked about his third prong, which was that they should learn how to calm not only their outward behavior but also their internal feelings. He thought yoga was good for that. And meditation. And tai chi. Then he actually had them stand up and do some deep breathing exercises complete with visual imagery, which Monica found utterly useless. Unfortunately, her relaxation of choice—a day at the spa— was pretty much out of the reach of her pocketbook these days.

When class was over, she headed to the Fireside Grill with Tonya and Susan. Going there after class had gotten to be such a routine that even when the classes were over they'd probably all head there at nine o'clock every Monday out of sheer force of habit. As a relaxation technique, it was pretty darned effective.

Tonya lit a cigarette and took a long drag. "I loved how Danforth told you that you should have been respectful to Jerry," she said to Monica. "I don't think he'd be telling you that if he knew why you were really so pissed at him."

"And please don't ever let him find out. Do I really want to hear that lecture?" She assumed his pompous voice. "Ms. Saltzman, perhaps you should consider the ramifications of your sexual behavior in relation to the workplace. Perhaps then anger issues would never come to the forefront."

"Wow," Tonya said. "You do Danforth better than Danforth does."

"So how are things going between you and Andi?" Susan asked.

Monica took a gulp of her martini before answering. "Does she have some kind of sixth sense or something? I can't do anything around that hospital without her knowing about it." She sighed. "I really would like to find another job."

"What's available at the hospital?" Tonya said.

"Not much. I've been trying to plant a few seeds here and there, but it's hard to do. Andi has a problem with me so much as talking to a man."

"What's wrong with doing that?" Susan said. "I talk to men at the hospital all the time." She smiled. "One man in particular."

Tonya turned to Monica. "She's going to be one of those nauseating women who gets all perky when they're in love, isn't she?"

"I'm not perky."

"Susan, you're so damned perky you make parakeets look depressed."

"Okay," she said. "So I'm perky."

Tonya turned to Monica. "She must have gotten laid."

"No, I didn't." That smile again. "Not yet."

She told them the story about her and Paul and their almost-nooner, and when she described the look on his face when he realized what *wasn't* going to happen, Monica grinned.

"Bet you're packing now, aren't you?" Tonya asked Susan.

"Yep. I've got a whole zipper pocket in my purse devoted to the cause." Her face fell a little. "But I am worried about what Lani's going to do when I finally tell her I'm seeing someone. She's just so miserable at the thought of me dating. All I did was mention that I talked to a man at a party, and already she thinks she's getting a stepfather. You should have seen how she flipped out. If she finds out I'm actually seeing Paul…well, it won't be pretty."

"Nobody likes change," Tonya said. "What else is new?"

"She needs my attention. If I'm dating a man, it might take my time away from her."

"So Lani's home all the time, and if you're not you won't have that quality time together?"

"Well, no, she's not home all the time."

"Tell her to go sleep over with a friend. Then *you* go sleep over with a friend."

"It's not that easy."

"She's fourteen," Monica said. "Has it ever occurred to you that she's just being a bratty teenage girl? That she'd be that way even if you and Don were Ward and June Cleaver?"

"I may be going out on a limb here," Tonya said, "but it looks to me as if she's feeding off your guilt. You feel like a rotten mother because of the divorce. Kids pick up on that. Basically, Susan, I don't think she's going to stop being miserable until you stop being miserable. So if seeing Paul, even under the radar, makes you happy, I say keep on doing it."

Susan smiled. "It does."

"Then don't you dare let anything come between you," Tonya said. "The good ones don't come along every day." She took a sip of her martini, then set it back on the table and turned away, a miserable frown on her face. Monica looked at Susan, and then they both looked back at Tonya. Something was up.

"So," Monica began. "How are things between you and Dale?"

"I'm still living over my shop. Does that tell you anything?"

"Have you seen him since that day you had the argument?"

"No. But—"

"What?"

Tonya paused, then shook her head. "It's probably nothing."

"It's clearly something," Susan said.

Tonya drained her martini. Staring down at her

empty glass, tears came to her eyes. She didn't seem to be one of those women who cried easily, so Monica hoped things weren't as bad as Tonya thought they were.

"I think Dale's going to file for divorce," Tonya said.

So much for something that wasn't bad.

"Now, wait a minute," Susan said. "What makes you think that?"

"Crystal, one of my stylists, came back from lunch on Friday and told me she saw Dale having lunch with his cousin."

"Well, that's not a problem unless it's a female cousin and his family boundaries are nonexistent," Monica said.

"Will you let me finish? It was his cousin Larry."

"Still not a problem."

"Larry is a divorce lawyer."

Monica raised her eyebrows. "Oh."

"So what do you think? Should I worry?"

"I don't know," Susan said. "How often do they have lunch together?"

"Maybe once every couple of months."

"No big deal, then," Susan reassured her. "It's just a coincidence."

"No," Tonya said. "I think the timing says something."

"Hmm." Susan said. "Well, there's one way to find out what's going on."

"How?"

"Ask Dale."

"Right. You want me to walk right up to him and say, 'Hey, honey, are you and Larry getting ready to take me to the cleaners?'"

"Either he's thinking of filing for divorce, or he isn't," Monica said. "If he isn't, you'll be relieved. If he is, it'll give you a chance to talk about it before things go too far."

Tonya nodded.

"Just talk to him," Susan said. "Calmly. Find out what's going on, and see where you go from there."

"I can't do it for at least a couple of days, because Dale's going to be working and I sure don't want to talk to him at the station."

"Then after that."

Tonya nodded again with uncharacteristic seriousness, and Monica actually felt sorry for her. It had to be hell to love a man so much that it ruled every waking thought and governed every emotion.

She thought about how her own love life had never been about love at all. It had been about getting what she wanted with a wink and a come-hither stare, with an ulterior motive underlying every move she made.

Sometimes when she was alone with nothing else to occupy her thoughts, she imagined what her life might be like if she'd taken a different path by marrying a nice but ordinary man and settling down the way most other women did. With the hindsight she had now, she was starting to feel as if she might have followed the wrong paradigm and missed something very precious along the way.

But regrets didn't do her much good at this point. At age forty-three, what were the odds that a nice man would wander along, one who didn't have a trunkful of baggage she wouldn't want to deal with? And having children in their forties might be an option for some women, but Monica couldn't even begin to get her mind around that.

She downed the last of her martini, washing those thoughts away. How crazy was it for her to think about relationships like that when she was having such a hard time getting her own life in order?

Monica stayed with Susan and Tonya for a while longer, then left the bar. She arrived home and grabbed her mail on her way in. When she tossed the envelopes on her dining room table, scattering them, she saw that the pile included some of the same bills that came every month. Only now a particularly ominous atmosphere surrounded them.

One from her mortgage company stood out in particular.

She sank to a chair, stared at the envelope for a moment, then looked away with a heavy sigh. The payment hadn't seemed like much when she'd worked at the bank. Now, though, her salary at the hospital barely covered it once her other bills were paid. If she didn't find a better-paying job soon, she'd have no choice but to sell her condo.

She remembered the huge shot of self-esteem she'd felt five years ago when she'd finally been able to buy a place of her own, and now she was getting ready to lose it. Pretty soon she'd be heading back to those department store bargain racks, because even apartment rent would eat up a large part of her current salary. She'd be doing all the things she'd been doing before she'd gone to work for Jerry, living the pitiful lifestyle she thought she'd said goodbye to forever.

For a moment she thought about her cousin, Sandra, and the way she always called her in the middle of the night to whine about her problems. Monica thought now might be a good time to call and whine about a few problems of her own. After all, Sandra owed her one. Hell, Sandra owed her twenty.

Maybe Danforth hadn't been so far off after all.

But the truth was that whining wasn't going to solve the problems Monica was facing now. She didn't know exactly what rock bottom was supposed to feel like, but she was pretty sure this was it.

CHAPTER 13

All the desperation Monica had felt the night before was still hanging on the next morning, but as she drove to work she told herself that the battle wasn't over yet. In any case, she wasn't going down without a fight.

Andi was out of the office all afternoon, which gave Monica the opportunity to join two doctors for a mid-afternoon coffee break in the cafeteria, then "accidentally" have a chat with the chief of staff while he was on his way to a regularly scheduled board meeting. Monica had a Ph.D. in ego stroking, so engaging him in conversation had been one of the easier things she'd ever done. And she'd managed to get a quick peek inside the boardroom, where she saw a couple of faces she recognized—Stan Goldblum and Edward Jernigan—men whose companies did business with First Republic Bank who were apparently on the hospital's board of directors. She made a mental note to find out the names of the rest of the board members to see if there was anyone worth focusing on there. In a short period of time, she'd planted some seeds for the future. With luck, one of them would sprout.

She only hoped it would happen before she lost everything.

She got off the elevator on the second floor and hurried toward her office, hoping she had beaten Andi back. No such luck. When she rounded the doorway, Andi was standing at Monica's desk, her eyebrows pulled together in a heavy scowl.

"Where have you been?"

Monica tried to think fast, but Andi had caught her off guard. "Uh...the bathroom?"

"Where are the presentation handouts you were preparing for me?"

Oh, boy. She'd forgotten all about those. "I'm just about finished," she lied. "Just another few hours—"

"I told you I wanted them by two o'clock today. I expected them by two o'clock today."

"I'm sorry," Monica said. "Give me an hour and I'll have them for you."

"This isn't the first time something like this has happened. Last week you were late with the monthly report."

"The copier was down."

"For an hour. That was all."

"Because I sweet-talked the repair guy into coming right over."

"Which cost the hospital a rush charge, which

wouldn't have been necessary if you hadn't been in a hurry to get the copying done because you were pushing your deadline. And look at that stack of filing," she said, nodding toward the top of one of the file cabinets.

"A lot of that was here when I got here. I'm just now starting to make a dent in it."

"You even screwed up the coffee this morning. There were grounds in it because you didn't get the filter in straight."

"Anybody can make a mistake."

"You're right. And that doesn't bother me a bit, as long as it's an honest mistake. But if the mistake is made because that employee just doesn't give a damn whether she does the job right or not, then it's not okay."

Monica didn't have a thing to say to that.

"And another thing. If you think you're gonna move in on the chief, think again."

Monica's mouth fell open. How did she *know* these things?

"I admit he's a good candidate," Andi said. "He already cheats on his wife. But you know what? He needs to stop doing that. And you need to stop doing what you're doing, too."

Monica was flabbergasted.

"Come into my office," Andi said.

Oh, God. What now?

Monica followed her. Andi shut the door and sat

down behind her desk, motioning Monica to one of her guest chairs. Monica braced herself for the harsh lecture she knew was coming. Strangely, though, Andi's usual tough-as-nails expression seemed to have disappeared, replaced by one of concern.

"Monica, do you realize that if you spent the same time and effort learning the job and doing the work as you did trying to kiss up to men in power at this hospital, you'd be a candidate for all kinds of opportunities?"

Monica gave her the barest of shrugs, because the truth was that she hadn't thought about that at all.

"At your age," Andi went on, "why are you still somebody's assistant? Why aren't you in a job where you have an assistant of your own?"

Monica had never considered that, and the comment hurt more than she would have thought. She swallowed hard, wishing she could hate Andi for saying it.

But she was speaking the truth.

Suddenly Monica felt inadequate in a way she never had before because, for the first time, she was facing a truth she'd tried desperately to ignore: twenty years had passed, and she had absolutely nothing to show for it. She was a forty-three-year-old woman doing a job the average twenty-three-year-old woman would be doing. And that was why Monica was making this kind of salary. She felt as if she'd chosen a fork in the road that led into a deep, dark forest she had no idea how to get out of. To her surprise, tears welled up in her eyes.

No. Stop it. Don't you dare cry.

But then she thought about that awful man she'd interviewed with in that horrible office, who'd shoved her aside in favor of a younger woman, and the tears kept coming.

Andi reached around, pulled a tissue out of a box and handed it to Monica.

"No. I don't need—"

"Take it."

Monica took it and dabbed away the tears.

"You can do this job with your eyes closed," Andi said. "Why in the world don't you?"

"I—" Monica tried to talk, but her throat was so tight her voice choked. "I don't know."

"You're bright, you're confident and you're good with people. But you don't put any of that to good use. Your age is already a detriment to most employers, even though they're not supposed to take that into account. And your lack of job skills is most definitely a detriment that they're well within their rights to hold against you. But I'm giving you a chance, Monica. A chance to back up and take the right path. It's up to you to decide if that's what you want to do."

Monica stared at her lap, her head pounding because she was trying so hard not to cry, which only muddled her thoughts even more than they already were.

"But I can't wait for that decision forever," Andi went on. "I've cut you some slack because of Susan, but you're not riding on her reputation any longer. So here's the bottom line. Two weeks. That's all you've got. Unless I see substantial improvement in your job performance, I'm going to have to let you go. Do you understand?"

Monica looked up at Andi, swallowing hard. In spite of the ultimatum she'd just issued, she wore an expression that was actually sympathetic. And that made Monica feel even worse.

"I know it's a little early to leave for the day," Andi said, checking her watch, "but you can go home if you want to. Just think about what I've told you, okay?"

Monica nodded, glad she wasn't going to have to sit out there with tears rolling down her face. She rose from the chair and left Andi's office to get her purse from her desk. Dabbing at her eyes some more, she tried to work up a fantasy of having a job as assistant to the chief of staff, getting the guy under her thumb, and then finding a way to lord it over Andi.

But she couldn't.

I'm giving you a chance to back up and take the right path.

Monica squeezed her eyes closed, her temples throbbing. Working here was the right path? She had such a hard time getting her brain around that. The pay was lousy, the environment bland and basic, and the boss so stern that it made Monica nervous just to be around her.

Then again, up until now she'd thought the path her mother had prescribed was the right one, and look how that had turned out. The moment she'd hurled that flowerpot through Jerry's windshield, all the security she'd thought she had vanished. She'd structured her life on such a flimsy foundation that she might never feel safe again.

She grabbed her purse and left the office, taking a different route out of the hospital than usual so she wouldn't pass by the E.R. Monica hadn't anticipated Susan becoming such a good friend, one who would go out on a limb to help her get her a job. What would Susan say now if she found out she was on the verge of losing it?

Monica went to the parking lot and got into her car. She sat in silence for a moment, looking back through the glass doors into the hospital lobby. She saw a nurse pushing a man in a wheelchair. A woman wearing a business suit standing by the entrance talking on a cell phone. A couple of white-coated men carrying on a conversation. They probably all had solid, well-paying jobs where they got some respect. And it was also quite possible that none of them had slept with anyone to get them.

As Monica watched the hospital employees come and go, her confusion began to fade, her mind becoming clearer. Maybe the "right path" Andi was talking about led to a place where she could wake up in the morning, go to work and feel good about her accomplishments, no matter how meager they were.

And now, for some reason, when Monica thought about Andi she seemed less like an adversary and more like the kind of person whose respect it might be worth it to have.

The next morning Monica was standing at the file cabinet, making a sizable dent in the "to be filed" stack when Andi got to the office. She greeted Monica as she usually did, with a mumbled "morning," as she headed for the coffeepot. She looked around for the disposable cups before spying a pair of ceramic mugs.

She picked one up and looked at Monica. "What are these?"

"I hate drinking out of foam cups."

"Who's going to keep these clean?" she asked.

"I am."

Andi looked at her with confusion, then turned to the coffeepot and wrinkled her nose. "And what kind of coffee is this?"

"Something that won't eat a hole through the bottom of the pot for a switch. That coffee you have here is hideous. I've seen you eat those raspberry Danishes from the cafeteria, so—" she gave a little shrug "—I thought you'd like raspberry coffee."

Andi poured a cup and stared down at it, her nose

still crinkled. Then she took a sip, and her eyebrows rose with surprise.

"Good?" Monica said.

Her face went impassive again. "It's okay." Then she looked at the report on the corner of Monica's desk. "You typed this?"

"Yes."

"You didn't talk somebody into doing it for you?"

"It's my job. Of course I did it myself. Look it over, and I'd be happy to do any revisions."

Andi stared at her as if she'd grown an extra head. She picked up the report and started back to her office, only to see the philodendron Monica had grabbed out of her living room this morning.

"What's that?"

"I thought this office could use a little cheering up."

Andi pondered that for a moment. "Hmm. I suppose it can stay. As long as you water it."

Andi's gaze panned around the office, focusing on the "to be filed" pile that was almost gone, the plant, the cups, the report and then back to Monica. "You seem to think you're going to be staying around here for a while."

"Yes, ma'am, I do."

For maybe the first time since Monica started working there, Andi did the unthinkable. She smiled. Or at least Monica thought it might be a smile. The edge of her mouth definitely twitched.

"Well, then. Carry on."

With that, Andi turned around, walked into her office and closed the door behind her.

Monica sat back in her chair with a heavy sigh. She'd had to rush like crazy to get everything done before Andi got here this morning. Typing that report had been the worst. Monica was definitely going to have to concentrate on increasing her typing speed.

She thought about the call she was going to be making this afternoon to a real estate agent to list her condo for sale. The very thought of it made her sick, but it had to be done. She had some never-worn clothes in her closet she was going to return, and she'd given up on the plans she'd had of replacing her five-year-old car with a new one this spring. With those changes and a few more, she could make it on this salary. Barely.

But she told herself things would get better. That getting by on her own hard work meant she could determine the direction of her own life. Still, it was going to be an uphill battle, one she didn't look forward to in the least. She just hoped in the end it would all be worth it.

It was noon on Thursday before Tonya finally got up the nerve to talk to Dale. She kept hoping and praying that he'd come to her to tell her he was sorry for what he'd done and that he loved her and only her. If only he'd meet her halfway, they could get past this.

But he hadn't. And that meant she had to do something or go crazy.

She felt nervous as all get-out when she pulled up in front of the house because it didn't even look like her house anymore. It looked like a place where Dale lived and she didn't.

She got out of the car and went to the door. She almost knocked, but that would have seemed really weird so instead she unlocked the door and went inside. A few moments later, Dale appeared at the doorway to the hall. He didn't look all that surprised to see her. He didn't look mad. And he sure didn't look like he was glad she was there. Then she realized that there was no emotion on his face period, and maybe that was the worst thing of all.

"Hi, Dale."

"What are you doing here?"

"Can we talk a minute?"

"I was just on my way out the door," he said.

To see another woman.

It drove Tonya crazy how her mind kept filling in all those words she swore were in Dale's head that he just wasn't saying.

"I only need a few minutes. I want to ask you about something."

Dale went to the rack near the door and grabbed his coat. "Okay," he said, putting it on. "A few minutes is about all I've got."

For you.

More filling in. Why did her brain have to keep doing that?

Even though Dale was standing close to her, she felt as if he was ten miles away. It hadn't been that long ago that she could have just taken a step forward, put her arms around his neck and given him a kiss. Then, if the time was right—and sometimes even it wasn't—he would have dragged her straight to the bedroom.

Now he just stood there, saying nothing. Looking at her as if she were a stranger.

"Crystal told me she saw you having lunch with Larry the other day."

"Oh, Crystal told you that, did she? That doesn't surprise me. Apparently she's made it her life's work to keep tabs on me."

Tonya ignored the comment, trying not to get upset, even as her hands were starting to shake. She shoved them into her coat pockets.

"Why were you having lunch with him?" she asked.

"Why do I always have lunch with Larry? He's my cousin. We have lunch a lot."

"Larry…" She couldn't say it.

"What?"

"Larry's a divorce lawyer."

For a few seconds, Dale just stared at her. "Are you telling me you thought…" He shook his head with disbelief. "Tonya, never in my life have I seen somebody jump to conclusions the way you do."

"So you weren't talking to him about getting a divorce?"

"Of course not. We were just having lunch."

"Maybe you just don't want to tell me to my face," Tonya said. "But I promise I won't go nuts or anything. I swear. I just want to talk about it."

"Didn't you hear me? I told you I wasn't—"

"Please," she said, squeezing her eyes closed. "I just need to *know*."

"Tonya. I told you I never talked to Larry about divorce." Then his face grew hard, and a strange light entered his eyes. "But maybe I should."

Tonya felt as if the earth had opened up and swallowed her, dragging her right down into some horrible place she'd never wanted to go.

"In three years of marriage, I've never crossed the line you said I did, yet for weeks now I've had to defend myself, anyway. And nothing's changed. All you'll tell me is that you're willing to forgive me for something I never did in the first place. Well, honey, that's not good enough."

Tonya bowed her head, swallowing hard and trying desperately not to cry. "I don't want a divorce."

"Why not? You divorced your last husband for cheating. If you think that's what I did, what's stopping you from divorcing me?"

Tonya had no idea what to say. That was the question she'd been trying so hard to answer all this time. Why, when she was so certain about what happened, didn't she just leave him for good?

For weeks now, she'd thought the most terrible thing that could happen was for her to believe him, only to have him cheat on her again. But now she realized that there might be something worse than that. What if she couldn't bring herself to believe him and it turned out he'd been telling the truth all along? Torn between those two possibilities, she felt paralyzed.

She couldn't believe him, but she couldn't leave him, either. It was a horrible stalemate she had no idea how to get out of.

Dale opened the door to leave the house, and Tonya grabbed his arm. "Dale. Please don't go. I want to work this out."

She held her breath, staring into those beautiful brown eyes, looking for something that would tell her, with absolute certainty, that he loved her and only her, he always had and he always would. Instead, his gaze hardened and the light seemed to disappear from his eyes.

"I'm not sure that's possible anymore."

Oh, God. No. Please don't say that.

"Even if we come to some kind of understanding now," Dale went on, "even if you were to say you believe me, I'm afraid another day's going to come when you'll see something suspicious, or one of your girlfriends will tell you something, and the accusations will start all over again. I can't live with a woman who doesn't trust me, Tonya. I won't."

With that, he left. Tonya just stood there, tears streaming down her face, holding on to only the thinnest thread of hope that Dale wouldn't be giving his cousin a call and ending their marriage once and for all.

CHAPTER 14

Monica had hoped that letting Andi know she intended to get serious about the job might make the woman let up on her. No such luck. Yesterday afternoon and again today, Andi had given her tasks that kept her busy every moment, some so challenging that Monica was sure she was going to fail. But she undertook them without complaint. One way or another, she had to get past that two weeks of probation and keep this job.

About three o'clock, Andi sent Monica on an errand to medical records, which gave her the chance to get out of the office and take a breather.

Passing by the hospital gift shop, she eyed the five-foot-tall teddy bear in the window wearing a T-shirt that said Grin And Bear It, wondering what kind of parent would actually buy that for a child. Then her gaze drifted to the counter, and she couldn't believe who she saw.

Edward Jernigan?

It made sense she would see him here; he was on the hospital's board of directors. But was it really him?

She started to walk right past the shop, but curiosity got the better of her. She stepped inside and up to the counter, pretending to examine a point of purchase display so she could look at him out of the corner of her eye.

It was him. No doubt about it. The tall, silver-haired, well-dressed chief operating officer of Wyatt Industries was standing right next to her. Whenever he came to the bank to do business with Jerry, he always stopped at her desk to chat, calling her by name and complimenting her on whatever happened to catch his eye that day—her hair, her dress, even her smile. Although he had to be pushing sixty, Edward was still a handsome man, especially since he spared no expense on clothing and personal fitness.

As he paid for a small bottle of aspirin, she casually glanced up at him, then did a phony double take.

"Mr. Jernigan?"

He turned, looking confused for a moment, then smiled. "Monica! What a surprise."

"It's a surprise to see you, too. What brings you to the hospital?"

"Business."

"Business?"

He dropped his voice. "Just between you and me, we had some contention at our last board of directors meeting, so I came here to discuss a few things with the chief of staff." He held up the aspirin. "I'm afraid the problems still aren't solved."

"That's too bad."

"We'll get there eventually." The clerk handed him his change, which he put in his pocket. "I was in First Republic the other day on business and was surprised when Jerry told me you no longer work there."

Oh, God. She could only imagine what else Jerry had told him. "Yes," she said tentatively. "That's right."

"So where are you working now?"

"Well, actually, I'm working here."

"Oh? Doing what?"

"I'm assistant to the director of nursing."

Jernigan's eyes widened. "Andi Shaunessy?"

"That's right."

He feigned a smile. "Uh…lovely woman. Do you enjoy working for her?"

Enjoy working for Andi? Monica couldn't imagine the day would ever come when she could say that and mean it, but the last thing she needed to be doing right now was saying anything negative behind Andi's back.

"Uh…yes. Actually, I do enjoy working for her."

Jernigan frowned. "Oh. That's a pity."

"Excuse me?"

"I had this thought…"

"Yes?"

He motioned for her to move away from the counter until they were standing alone.

"Tell me, Monica," he said. "Just how devoted are you to your current position?"

Monica's heart skipped. "Why do you ask?"

"My assistant is leaving next week. Would you be interested in interviewing for the job?"

For a moment, Monica was speechless. Would she be interested in working for Edward Jernigan, one of the most wealthy and influential businessmen in Dallas? Was he *joking*?

"Why, yes. Of course I'd be interested."

"I've been interviewing for nearly a month now, but I can't seem to find the right person. If you'd come by the office tomorrow, maybe we could discuss the position. What time do you get off work here?"

"Four-thirty."

"Could you make it by five?"

"Yes. Of course."

"Perfect. My office is on the fifty-third floor of the Wright Building. Do you know where that is?"

"Yes."

"Excellent," he said. "I'll see you tomorrow at five."

He turned and walked out of the gift shop, leaving Monica reeling with disbelief.

Wait. She had to think about this. It didn't make any sense. Jerry was the kind of guy to blackball her to anyone who would listen, yet he hadn't told Jernigan that she was fired and why?

As unbelievable as it seemed, it didn't look as if he had. Otherwise Jernigan wouldn't be asking her to interview for the job. And his asking her personally could mean only one thing: barring anything unforeseen, the job would be hers.

Monica closed her eyes for a moment, basking in the thought of working at a place where her heels sank into plush carpet. Where solid cherrywood file cabinets swooshed closed. Where the company piped in classical music that could soothe any soul.

And her condo. She'd thought she was going to have to say goodbye to it forever, but now she felt a rush of hope that she wouldn't have to after all. There was still time to call off the real estate agent.

I'm giving you a chance to back up and take the right path.

Andi's words suddenly popped into Monica's mind, and for a moment she felt a twinge of guilt. She had no delusions about what a job working for a man like Jernigan might entail. Just the way he looked at her told her she'd likely be earning her salary in more places than just the office.

But she didn't know that for sure. And it certainly wouldn't hurt to go to his office tomorrow and see what he had to offer. Yeah, Andi's words had sounded noble, but that was because Monica had no other options at the time.

Now she did.

At five o'clock the next evening, Monica was riding the elevator to the fifty-third floor of the Wright Building. As it ascended, she got that swooping feeling in her stomach that she always did in elevators that went so fast because they had so high to go.

The doors opened, and ahead was a pair of heavy oak doors with a brass plate that read, Wyatt Industries. Just that much expensive hardwood in one place was enough to make Monica swoon.

She pushed the door open and walked into the office. The first thing she saw was a reception desk, oak with a granite top, polished to a high sheen. Framed watercolors lined the walls, with each piece spotlighted individually. The scents of fine wood, leather furniture and plush carpeting mingled together and drifted into her nostrils. She took a deep, furtive breath, feeling as if she'd finally come home.

A stunning green-eyed blonde sat behind the reception desk, and as Monica approached the woman acknowledged her with a simple lift of her eyebrows.

"Hello. I'm Monica Saltzman. I have an appointment with Mr. Jernigan."

"Go right in," she said, nodding toward a partially closed door. "He's expecting you."

Monica walked over and pushed the door open, easing her head inside. Jernigan looked up from his desk and smiled.

"Monica. Come in."

She stepped into his office and was astonished by its size. Situated in a corner of the building, two of the walls were solid glass, offering a stunning view of

Dallas. His desk was huge and well-appointed. A wet bar, no doubt stocked with every premium liquor made, lined part of one wall. Along another sat a sofa crafted of fabric that had to have cost a hundred dollars a yard.

Jernigan came around his desk and led her to the sofa. "Have a seat."

She sat down on that impossibly rich and decadent sofa, feeling as if she were sinking into a cloud.

"I'll get right to the point," Jernigan said. "I was happy to learn that you were no longer with First Republic. It appears that Jerry Womack's loss just may be my gain."

Monica almost melted with delight.

"And just between you and me—" Jernigan leaned closer and dropped his voice "—I think you were quite justified in doing what you did."

"Uh...doing what I did?"

"Putting that flowerpot through the windshield of Jerry's Hummer. That was absolutely inspired."

Monica was stunned. Jerry had actually told him that? And Jernigan thought it was *inspired?*

"A Hummer," Jernigan said with disgust. "Really. A man who drives one of those is clearly compensating for something. And then to shove you aside for a younger woman. He actually admitted as much. More compensation, don't you think?"

Monica just smiled. This was going too well for her

to mess it up with the wrong comment about Jerry's manhood. Or lack thereof.

"Pardon me for being so blunt," Jernigan said, "but in my opinion, Jerry Womack is an idiot."

Jerry is an idiot. At the sound of those words, Monica felt like dancing. She couldn't *wait* to rub his nose in this. Maybe she'd see him at Fireside Grill again with sweet little Nora and just happen to drop the bomb that she was working for a man with more power and prestige than he could ever hope to have. A man who thought he was an idiot for dumping her. *Ha. Take* that *Jerry.*

"He's not a lot younger than I am," Jernigan said, "and yet he has that foolish mentality that a twenty-something woman is preferable to one with more experience."

"Well, I'm glad you think so, Mr. Jernigan."

"I can't have just any woman representing me. It has to be a woman who knows what's required in an environment like this. How to deal with important people. She has to have style to go along with the substance."

Then he named a salary figure, and Monica almost fell off the sofa. She wasn't making anywhere near that much at the hospital. She hadn't made anywhere near that much at the bank. She'd never imagined making that much *ever.*

"Does that figure sound fair to you?" he asked.

"Yes, of course," she said, trying not to sputter. "More than fair."

"Then you're accepting my offer?"

Did he actually think she would say no? "Of course. I think we're going to get along very well."

"Yes. I believe we are, too." His gaze drifted down to her breasts. "After all, I've always thought you were a very beautiful woman."

Monica froze. She'd gotten so caught up in the salary and the stunning office that she'd forgotten for a moment what was at the heart of Jernigan's offer.

"I'm a very generous man," Jernigan said, his eyes roving down the length of her legs and back up again. "And from what Jerry has told me in the past, you're an equally generous woman."

Monica felt a sinking sensation in her stomach. Now she knew for sure what men discussed during all those three-martini lunches, and it had nothing to do with business. But sitting there now in that gorgeous office, her thoughts traveled back to the money she was going to be making that she desperately needed, and somehow a provocative smile found its way across her face.

"You have no idea how generous I can be."

The words came out of her mouth, but it was as if someone else had spoken them, some long-lost woman who'd taken a turn in a direction she never should have and was destined to stay on that path forever.

No. Stop it. You're getting what you always wanted, aren't you?

"How much notice do you have to give at your current job?" Jernigan asked.

Notice? Andi would probably be happy to boot her out the door anytime she was willing to go.

"I'm not sure. Would it be all right if I got back to you on that?"

"Of course. But I would like to have you on board in three weeks. I have some business to attend to in New York, and I want you to come along. I hope you like New York?" He smiled knowingly. "Fifth Avenue is beautiful this time of year."

Shop till you drop, sweetheart. I might even be willing to pick up the tab. Of course, you'll pay for it in other ways.

Monica forced a smile. "What woman doesn't love New York?"

Strangely, there was nothing lewd about any of this. It was simply the kind of interaction that occurred between two people who each had an agenda, and those agendas had converged. It was a small price to pay for being back in familiar territory, where she knew how to play the game.

Jernigan walked with her to the door and said he was looking forward to hearing from her about when she could start. She nodded and smiled, thanked him and left, not even acknowledging the receptionist as she walked out of the office.

The elevator came quickly. She leaned against the wall as it descended, her shoulders tense, her hand clutching her shoulder bag in a fierce grip.

Wrong path, wrong path, wrong path...

The words pounded inside her head, jabbing at her conscience, telling her that once she got off this elevator she should never get on it again. But by the time it reached the ground floor, she'd stood up straight and got herself back under control.

She was being given a second chance to use the only talents God had ever blessed her with, and she'd be a fool to pass it up.

During the time Paul was away, Susan went to Victoria's Secret and bought matching bras and panties, and for the first time in her life, she came away with colors other than white or beige. She tested every perfume at a department store counter until she found the perfect one. She bought bubble bath and soaked in the tub for an hour, then gave herself a manicure and pedicure. It had been years since she'd done any girly stuff at all, and it felt good to finally do something just for herself. Of course, Lani thought she'd lost her mind because her experience told her that Mom just didn't do things like that, which made doing them that much more fun.

Paul had called her every day he was gone just to chat. The day before he was due back at work, he reminded her of their plans for Saturday night, as if there was any way she could possibly forget.

Because Lani was spending the weekend with Don, Susan had all day Saturday to get ready. By the time Paul finally arrived at her house that night, she thought she was going to burst with excitement. He took her to dinner at a quiet steakhouse, and over a wonderful filet and a really nice glass of wine she learned more about his family, his daughters, his life. She shared her recent ups and downs with Lani. He told stories about his own daughters when they were Lani's age, and when he swore that they really did grow out of the teenage angst it gave Susan hope for the future.

Later, when they left the restaurant to go to the movie, she realized she hadn't been to a theater with a man in ages. Don had always preferred renting, which was fine most of the time, but there was nothing like sitting in a darkened theater with a man you were crazy about, snuggling close, sharing popcorn, whispering about the film and occasionally sharing a kiss or two. The fact that they were watching a really edgy thriller only compounded the fun.

About halfway through the movie, Susan started to think about what was going to happen afterward. Tonight, nothing was going to stop them from finishing what they'd started that lunch hour at Paul's house, and she couldn't wait.

When the movie was over, they came down the stairs from the upper part of the theater, stopping for the people in front of them to exit their row. As they waited, Paul slipped his arm around her shoulders and gave her a kiss.

"Mom?"

Susan froze. *Oh, God. This can't be happening.* She turned around slowly.

Lani.

As shocked as she was to see her daughter, Lani was equally shocked to see her mother.

With a man.

Who was kissing her.

CHAPTER 15

For a moment, Susan couldn't think straight. It just didn't compute that Lani was here. At an R-rated movie. At ten o'clock at night. Susan looked back and forth between Lani and her friend Kaylee, who had no more business being there than Lani did.

They stepped aside, allowing other people to pass, and then Susan focused on Lani again. "Why aren't you with your father?"

Lani stared at Paul, her eyes falling into a suspicious stare. "Kaylee asked me to stay over, and Dad said it was okay."

"What are you doing at this movie? It's rated R."

"Kaylee's mom got us in when she dropped us off."

Which was why Susan always thought twice about letting Lani do anything with Kaylee. And hadn't she discussed that with Don about a million times? Did he *ever* listen to her?

But when Lani's suspicious stare intensified, Susan realized she had a far bigger problem than her daughter watching a film inappropriate for her age.

"Honey," Susan said carefully, "this is Mr. White. He's a friend of mine."

"No," Lani said. "He's not just a friend. I saw you kissing!"

"Please keep your voice down," Susan said.

"I told you this was going to happen! Didn't I tell you?"

"Lani—"

"First Dad, and now you? Doesn't anybody think about *me?*"

"Honey, let me take you home so we can talk about this, okay?"

"No! I'm staying with Kaylee. Her mom's picking us up."

"Lani—"

"I don't ever want to talk to you again!"

With that, she spun around and stormed off, with Kaylee following close behind her.

Susan just stood there, shaking her head in disbelief. The elation she had felt at being with Paul was slowly being displaced by the terrible feeling that she'd just scarred her daughter for life.

Almost everyone had left the theater, so Susan just sank back down into a nearby chair. "I am *so* sorry about this. I had no idea we'd run into her."

Paul sat down beside her. "Hey, I raised two girls of my own. I'm used to their subtle displays of emotion."

"I feel like such a lousy mother."

"You're not a lousy mother. Stop beating yourself up."

"It's just so hard to see her miserable and know I was the cause of it."

"Take it easy. She'll get over it."

"Don't bet on that."

"Susan, she can never get used to the idea of you having a life of your own if you never give her the chance. Now you're giving her the chance."

"But it's tearing her up. First she found out Don and Marla are getting married, and now she thinks she's losing her mother, too."

"So do you expect Don to cancel his engagement?"

"Of course not."

"Why not? That would make Lani happy."

"I can't control what Don does. But I can control what I do."

"Why in the world should you have to? Just let her learn to deal with it."

She turned and dropped her forehead against his shoulder with a muffled groan of sheer frustration. He pulled her into a hug, and that only made things worse because it made her feel so good when she knew she should be feeling bad.

"Tell me now, Susan. Is this going to come between us?"

It should. If she was any kind of devoted mother at all, she'd rise to that wonderful level of nobility where she put her child first, even if it meant suffering herself.

But something inside her didn't buy that completely. There had to be a middle ground.

"No," she told Paul. "Of course not. I have to deal with Lani. I just wish I knew how."

"I wish I could tell you how, but I'm fresh out of advice."

"I remember what she was like before the divorce," Susan said. "So sweet and compliant. One of those kids who was never any trouble."

"She changed after you and Don broke up?"

"It was like she was a different person."

Yeah, she'd become a different person, all right. Like a grizzly bear coming out of hibernation that you'd better not poke with a stick. Then Don's engagement had made things worse, but it ended up being Susan who had to deal with Lani's resentment about that. It was as if the two of them were running from that grizzly bear, but because Don had gotten a head start Susan was the one getting eaten.

If only Don would take some of the responsibility for dealing with their daughter, things would be so much easier. Tonight was a good example. He'd taken the easy way out and let her hang out with Kaylee again without questioning what they were doing, and they'd ended up at an R-rated movie. He'd turned into more of a favorite uncle than a father, taking all the good and leaving Susan all the bad. And since he'd never been much of an authority figure in the first place, he wasn't about to step up to the plate on any issue.

So, as always, it was all up to her.

"You'll figure this out," Paul said. "As long as you remember that you're just as entitled to be happy as the rest of your family is."

Maybe so. But somehow there never seemed to be enough happiness to go around, and Susan was the one who always got left out.

"I just don't know what to do now," Susan said, feeling lost. "Maybe I should go to Kaylee's house."

"Hmm. To do what? Drag her away from her friend's house and take her home to talk to her about something she doesn't want to talk about in the first place? Uh…I'm thinking she'll be less than receptive to that."

Susan sighed. He had a point.

"I swear I'm not saying that just because I want you all to myself tonight." He paused. "Okay, that's part of it. But Lani still wouldn't appreciate it."

He gave her a smile, and part of that elation that had slipped away returned again.

"You're right," Susan said. "It's better to let her cool off. I'll talk to her when Don brings her home tomorrow."

"Good idea."

"I'll need to call Don in the morning and let him know what he might be in for when he picks Lani up at Kaylee's house."

Paul nodded, and she rubbed her hand over his. "I may not be very good company tonight."

"Don't worry. I promise I'll take your mind off all of this." He leaned over to whisper in her ear. "Did I tell you I have a hot tub?"

They left the movie theater, and on the way to Paul's house Susan put Lani out of her mind, concentrating instead on how heavenly that hot tub was going to be. But as it turned out, once they got there, Paul had barely closed the door behind them before he was pulling her into his arms.

"I've had a long time to think about this," Paul said. "Damn near killed me. Sorry, but the hot tub is going to have to wait."

When he caught her mouth with his, kissing her with the kind of enthusiasm that came from a heaping dose of delayed gratification, Susan was hardly complaining. They started toward his bedroom, unbuttoning one thing, then kissing, then pulling off something else, and by the time they got there Paul was shirtless and shoeless, and she was down to nothing but her new underwear. He reached into a nearby dresser drawer and pulled out a condom and tossed it onto the bed.

"And don't worry," Paul said. "There's plenty more where that came from."

"And I have plenty if you don't."

They grinned at each other, and in seconds he was out of his pants and was drawing her onto the bed with him. Soon she was on her back and he was kissing her, his hands roaming over her. He cupped his hand over her breast, pausing for a few second to test the lacy fabric of her bra with his fingertips.

"Mmm," he murmured. "Nice."

"Me or the bra?"

"Both."

Good answer.

He ran his hand along her abdomen, then slipped it beneath her panties, that silky little scrap of cloth she'd barely had the nerve to buy but now she was so very glad she had. And soon those were on the floor, too, and it was just the two of them naked together.

Now she knew how hungry she'd been for the taste and texture and warmth of male skin. Starving for it. She was starving for all of him, and that was what he gave her, grabbing the condom and ripping it open, and soon he was moving on top of her. When he slid inside, a little cry escaped her, maybe one of astonishment at just how good it felt. He made love to her with the eagerness of a man who had been denied too long, with strokes that were quick and sure and hard-driving. He whispered her name, his breath like fire against her neck.

"Susan," he said. "Too fast. I know it is. I just—"

"No," she said. "Do it now. *Now.*"

She didn't want it slow. She didn't want to break the crazy spell they'd been under since they'd hit his front door. She wanted to feel his lack of control, to feel how much he wanted her, to drive him over the top just as quickly as she could.

And a moment later, she did.

She loved the way his body tensed, the sound he made deep in his throat, the involuntary shudder that told her just how good it was.

For a while afterward, he lay on top of her, and she stroked his back, loving the feel of him beneath her hands. Finally he rolled away, his head falling to the pillow, and turned to look at her with a heavy-lidded expression of pure satisfaction.

"Too fast for you," he said again. "It had to have been."

"It wasn't about that this time. Not for me."

He rose on one elbow, kissed her lips, then the swell of her breast, as his hand skimmed her abdomen and lower.

"How about this time?" he whispered.

Her eyes drifted closed, her breath coming faster. As it turned out, not only did this man know what to say, he knew what to do, touching her in ways that sent her over the top before she knew it. When it was over, she wondered how she was going to make the feeble, boneless thing that her body had become ever walk again.

"I just want you to know," Paul said with mock gravity, "that I don't usually do this on the first date."

Susan laughed, unable to believe how good this was, that it had been so much better than she ever could have imagined.

"Don't worry," she told him. "I'll still respect you in the morning."

When he smiled and kissed her again, it made the whole experience feel like a gorgeous gift-wrapped package with a great big bow on top. She had the most glorious feeling that she still had it and a man still wanted it—a warm, wonderful man who made her feel the age she was in her mind rather than the age she really was. And that was the best gift of all.

As much as Susan was still worried about a confrontation with Lani, after tonight she knew just how important it was to convince her daughter how good her relationship was with Paul, and how, in the end, it was going to make all their lives better.

Susan was in her kitchen fixing dinner the next evening when she heard a car door slam outside. A few moments later, the front door opened and closed.

Lani was finally home.

Susan's heart skipped crazily in anticipation of what was coming. All afternoon she had imagined every scenario under the sun that might take place, and not one of them was good. There could be screaming. Crying. Long, horrible silences. She couldn't remember anything in recent memory she had wanted to deal with less.

Lani came into the kitchen and dumped her backpack beside the door. "Hi, Mom." She opened a cabinet and grabbed a couple of cookies. "What's for dinner?"

Susan blinked with surprise. Lani sounded calm. Pleasant. Nonconfrontational. Was this a new tactic? Disarm the enemy, then go for the throat?

"Hamburger noodle casserole," Susan said.

Lani bit into a cookie. "Good. I like that."

Okay, this was creepy. Was she waiting for Susan to bring it up so she could go ballistic? Maybe. But even at the risk of starting an argument, Susan couldn't avoid the issue.

"Look, Lani, about what happened last night…"

"You mean at the movie theater?"

"Yes."

Lani shrugged. "It's cool."

Susan froze with disbelief. "It doesn't bother you that I'm seeing Paul?"

"No."

"Uh…you were pretty upset about it when you left the theater last night."

"I thought about it and it's okay."

Something wasn't computing. Either the pod people had come in the past few hours and put an alien in Lani's place, or she was actually learning to think like an adult. Susan mulled that over for a moment and decided that her daughter had a lot of wonderful qualities, but being adultlike wasn't yet one of them.

Maybe there was something she wanted badly

enough that she was giving in now so her mother would cave on something later. And since this issue required a lot of concession on Lani's part, whatever she was planning to hit Susan with in the future was bound to be a doozy.

"Why don't you invite him to my basketball game?" Lani said.

Susan stared at her dumbly. Psychological warfare. It was the only explanation. "Are you sure about that? You don't even like it when Marla's there."

"I said I wanted him to come, didn't I?"

"Okay, then. I'll invite him. But why the change of heart?"

"I thought you wanted to see the guy."

"I do."

"Then why are you asking?"

"I—" Susan stopped short. Good question. "Never mind."

"Dad and Marla will be there, too, won't they?"

"As far as I know."

"Good. That'll be nice."

What had happened to *I hate Marla*?

Maybe Paul was right. Maybe Lani just needed time to get used to the idea of her parents having lives of their own. Could it be as simple as that?

Lani gave her a smile—an actual turning up of the corners of her mouth in a pleasant manner—and disappeared into her bedroom. Susan looked after her with total disbelief, then went to her own bedroom, picked up the phone and called Paul. He was happy things had worked out so well and was equally happy for the invitation to join them at the basketball game.

Susan hung up the phone, trying to shove aside her natural tendency to think that if something seemed too good, it probably was. But this seemed *way* too good to be true. After all, she was going to the basketball game next Wednesday with an attractive man who was sweet and affectionate and great in bed, and finally she wouldn't be warming the bleachers alone while Don and Marla sat hip to hip, holding hands and being cute.

She lay back on the bed and closed her eyes, imagining how wonderful that was going to be.

The next Monday afternoon, Tonya took care of her last customer and headed up to her apartment, feeling so exhausted that climbing the stairs was a chore. She went inside and locked the door behind her, collapsing on the sofa.

Forget the stairs. Even *breathing* was a chore. She'd always wondered what depression felt like. Now she knew.

She sat on the sofa in silence, replaying her last conversation with Dale in her mind, just as she had about a thousand times since then. All she wanted right now was to crawl into bed, pull the covers over her head and try to dream of better days, even though she had a feeling her better days had already happened and it was all downhill from here. Unfortunately, it was Monday, and anger management class was in an hour, which meant she had to sit through another two hours of Danforth.

She closed her eyes with a soft groan. No. She couldn't do it. She just couldn't. They were allowed to miss one class, and this one was going to be it.

She dug through the depths of her purse looking for Danforth's card, before upending the damned bag on her sofa and fishing through the pile of stuff. Finally she located the card and reached for the phone, only to have it ring before she could pick it up.

Her heart leaped into a crazy rhythm. *No. It's not him. You always think it could be him, but you know it's not so quit getting your hopes up.*

She took a deep, calming breath and answered it on the third ring. "Hello?"

"Tonya, this is Susan."

"Hi, Susan. What's up?"

"It's Dale."

Confused, Tonya sat up straighter and pressed the phone closer to her ear. "What? What about Dale?"

"I'm at the E.R. There was a four-alarm fire at an apartment complex tonight. Several people were injured, including two firefighters. Dale was one of them."

CHAPTER 16

Tonya's stomach was in a knot all the way to the hospital. She had a hard time driving carefully as Susan had told her to, mostly because the tears in her eyes made the road so blurry.

Dale had a head injury, Susan had told her, but he was conscious now. She said there was a good chance he didn't have any bleeding on his brain because his neurological exam was normal, but they wanted to do some tests to make sure. But Tonya watched shows like E.R. She knew doctors could find problems even when they thought there weren't any, and she wasn't going to believe he was okay until she saw him with her own eyes.

She parked her car and raced into the emergency room. Susan came out of the back before she could even get to the reception desk.

"Susan! What's going on? How is he?"

Susan sat her down in a chair in the waiting room. "They're taking him upstairs for a CT scan right now."

"What happened? What caused the accident?"

"He pulled two people out of that apartment

complex and was going in for a third when a beam collapsed and fell on him."

Tonya slid her hand to her throat at the thought that Dale could be dead right now. He'd done it again. He'd gone into a burning building one too many times. He had actually been reprimanded before for taking too many chances, and it was probably going to happen again.

Tonya heard footsteps and turned to see Monica approaching.

"Monica?" Tonya said. "What are you doing here?"

She sat down on the other side of Tonya. "Susan called and told me what happened. How's Dale?"

Susan filled her in on his condition, and then Monica said, "I got in touch with Danforth and told him if he went to class tonight he'd be talking to an empty room."

"He'll probably go anyway," Susan said. "The man does like to hear himself speak."

Monica and Tonya nodded in agreement. There was a long silence, broken only by a baby crying in the distance.

"I finally asked Dale about the lunch he had with his cousin," Tonya said.

Monica and Susan came to attention.

"He wasn't talking to him about a divorce. But then Dale and I had another awful fight. Even if he wasn't considering it before, he may be now."

Susan sighed. "Oh, sweetie. I'm so sorry."

"He tells me he can't live with a woman who doesn't trust him. But..."

"What?"

"After everything I've seen...after everything that's happened to me..." She took a deep, shaky breath. "I just don't know how to...."

Tonya's voice trailed off. Susan and Monica turned away, and Tonya knew why: they didn't have answers for her, either.

Then a woman in scrubs came into the waiting area.

"That's Dale's doctor," Susan said, and the three of them stood up. The doctor told them Dale was back from the CT scan, and it showed no abnormalities. They wanted to keep him overnight for observation because he had had a hard blow to the head, but he could probably go home sometime tomorrow.

Tonya almost fainted with relief. "Can I see him?"

"Room three-seventeen," she said. "They'll have him there shortly."

The doctor left, and Tonya hugged Susan and Monica. "Thanks for being here." She looked over her shoulder. "I—I guess I'll go see him now."

Susan squeezed her arm. "Everything's going to be okay, sweetie. You'll see."

It had to be. Somehow she and Dale had to get back to the way things were before all this happened because Tonya couldn't even imagine how her life was going to be if they didn't.

* * *

Monica waited until Tonya was out of earshot, then turned to Susan. "So what do you think? Do they have a prayer of staying together?"

Susan shook her head skeptically. "I don't know. Tonya's carrying around an awful lot of baggage."

"Do you think Dale really did cheat on her?"

"I don't know that, either. There's a lot of water under the bridge. They may have a hard time making things right again."

"Yeah, but Tonya's the kind of woman you shouldn't underestimate. If she wants everything to work out, I bet she'll find a way to make it happen."

Susan nodded her head in agreement. "So how are things going with you and Andi?"

Monica felt a twinge of guilt, then pushed it aside and put a smile on her face. "Actually, I'm leaving the hospital."

Susan's eyes widened. "You mean for good?"

"Yes." Monica kept smiling, but it felt phony. "I have another job offer."

"Really? Where?"

"Working for Wyatt Industries."

"I've heard of that company. That's great. What are you going to be doing?"

"I'm going to be executive assistant to the COO."

Susan's smile faded. "That's good."

"It's exactly the job I wanted. It's in a beautiful office

on the fifty-third floor of the Wright Building downtown. Gorgeous view. Expensive furnishings. Art on the walls. *Originals*."

"So how did you find out about this job?"

Monica laughed a little. "Funny thing. Edward Jernigan, my new boss, used to do business at the bank. Jerry was the one who told him I no longer worked there. He thinks Jerry was an idiot to fire me and wants me to come to work for him."

Susan nodded but then tilted her head and narrowed her eyes, as if she sensed something Monica wasn't saying.

"What?" Monica said.

"Nothing."

But it was pretty clear what she was thinking, and it really irritated Monica. "Go ahead, Susan. Ask."

"What?"

"Ask me who I screwed to get the job."

"I wasn't thinking that."

"Of course you were."

"Okay. Who did you screw to get the job?"

Monica hadn't counted on Susan behaving like Tonya. She turned away. "Nobody."

Susan kept staring at her.

"Yet."

"Monica!" Susan said, then glanced at the three people sitting along the opposite wall of the waiting area, who were suddenly all ears. She pulled Monica out the door and into the hall, lowering her voice. "Why do you keep on doing that? You have a perfectly good job here at the hospital!"

"Perfectly good? Working for Andi? Are you *kidding* me?"

"No. I'm not."

"Well, it doesn't really matter. She's probably going to fire me, anyway."

"What?"

"A few days ago, she put me on a two-week probation."

"Okay, she told me about that. But she also told me that since then you've been trying harder."

"No matter what I do, it'll never be enough for her."

"Look, I know she can be a little harsh in the way she relates to people, but she's as fair as anybody I've ever known. As long as she knows you're trying, she won't fire you."

"I don't even want that job. I mean, why would I, when I can make twice as much working somewhere else?"

"Because there are more important things than money."

Monica rolled her eyes. "Spare me the clichés, will you?"

"Let me get this straight. You don't want a decent, honest job. You'd rather sleep with a man you barely know and certainly don't love for the privilege of sitting in some museum of an office doing essentially nothing?"

"It's a very prestigious position!"

"Yeah, it's a position, all right," Susan said. "Missionary."

Monica shook with resentment. "Listen, Susan. You didn't come from where I came from. Nobody ever told me I had anything going for me *but* my looks. It started with beauty pageants when I was five. My mother told me to stand up straight, prance around and smile, smile, smile. It took me until I was about ten or eleven to read the smiles I was getting back from some of those perverted judges. But I was on a roll by then. Did you know I was once runner-up for Miss Texas?"

Susan just stared at her.

"My mother told me school was a waste of time when I could marry well. Somehow, though, that never happened. So I'm using the only talents I have to get the kinds of jobs that will give me a decent lifestyle. Edward Jernigan is going to be paying me more money than I've ever seen in my life, and I'm not about to turn it down."

"Yeah, money's nice," Susan said. "But there's a lot to be said for self-respect."

"Self-respect," Monica said, "is highly overrated."

With that, she yanked her purse up over her shoulder, spun around and headed for the front door of the hospital, thinking about how thrilled she was going to be the day she walked out of this place for the last time.

Tonya peeked into Dale's hospital room to see him tucked beneath a sheet and blanket, his eyes closed. She just stood there at the doorway for a minute, watching him, thinking about how he'd pulled two people out of that burning building only to get hurt himself. So many things about Dale were wonderfully good and right. So how could everything between them have gone so wrong?

She walked into the room. He turned at the sound of her footsteps and opened his eyes, his face tightening into a grimace.

"Hi," she said, sitting down in a chair by his bed. "Headache?"

"A little."

Judging from the look on his face, it was more like a lot. "Did they give you something for the pain?"

"Yeah. It's starting to kick in."

"A couple of people are alive tonight because of you. I think that makes you a hero."

"Come on, Tonya. It's just my job. It's like me saying you're a hero for giving somebody a really good haircut."

"Yeah, but unless I really slip with those scissors, nobody's exactly in a life-threatening situation."

She smiled. When she didn't get one in return, one more piece of her heart disintegrated.

"The doctors say you're going to be fine. That your CT scan was okay. You can probably go home tomorrow afternoon."

"Good."

"I'll take you home."

When he just stared at her, not smiling, she knew nothing had changed since she'd seen him last. They were still miles away from each other.

"Okay," he said finally, but his voice was hardly filled with enthusiasm. If the devil himself was standing in front of her right now, she'd sell her soul for a way to make things right again.

"It's late," Dale said, "and I'm pretty wiped out. We can talk again in the morning."

"Are you sure you don't need me to stay?" she asked.

"If I need something, there are nurses."

But they don't love you. That's the difference.

Finally she just nodded, wishing she could hold his hand. Kiss him. But she wouldn't be able to stand it if he pulled away.

She picked up her purse and started to stand, only to have a question she'd been thinking about for days now come back into her head.

"Dale?"

"Yeah?"

Maybe she shouldn't ask this. Maybe it would only

stir things up all over again. But she really wanted to know.

"What would you have done if you'd been me?" she asked him. "Say, if Cliff had called you to say he saw me leaving a bar with a guy and going home with him? What would you have done?"

"Nothing."

"Nothing?"

"What would be the point? I would already know nothing happened that I needed to worry about."

She looked at him imploringly. "But I don't understand. How would you *know* that?"

Dale looked at her through heavy-lidded eyes, speaking as if the answer were so crystal clear that everyone in the world knew it.

"It's faith, honey," he said. "And that's it."

And that's it.

She tried to get her brain around that, but blindly believing something when contrary evidence was right before her eyes had never made much sense to her. But Dale was no fool. Why did things come so easily to him that she couldn't understand if she lived to be a thousand?

Suddenly a loud voice boomed behind her. "Hey, you moron! You were supposed to duck!"

Tonya spun around to see Cliff coming into the room along with two of the other guys from the station. They mumbled a greeting to her, then went up to Dale's bed.

"Oh, yeah?" Dale said. "It's hard to duck a ceiling joist coming down."

"That's what happens when you play hero," Cliff said. "You cut it too close. The chief is probably going to have your ass for that."

And then the guys pulled up chairs and launched into their usual post-fire analysis, like a bunch of jocks after the big game. Even though Dale seemed to be drifting, he wasn't telling them to leave. She told herself that it was just one of those guy things, but she wasn't sure she believed it.

She wasn't sure, either, if he even noticed when she slipped out the door.

CHAPTER 17

When Monica arrived home she was still fuming, and she had no idea when it was going to stop. Susan had a hell of a lot of nerve talking to her like that. Monica was going to give her notice to Andi, then head up that elevator to the executive suite, where she'd live the high life she'd always dreamed of.

But the truth was that she'd had all day today to tell Andi she was leaving and she hadn't done it. Why?

Tomorrow. She'd tell her tomorrow.

Then she heard a knock. Who could be at her door at eight o'clock at night? She looked out the peephole.

Edward Jernigan?

She opened the door. He wore perfectly tailored slacks and a casual shirt, looking like a man who had lived with money all his life and wasn't afraid to spend it.

"Mr. Jernigan?"

"Aren't you going to invite me in?"

"Yes. Of course."

Monica stepped aside and he came into her condo.

"Why are you here?" she asked, closing the door behind him.

He shrugged. "I just happened to be in the neighborhood."

No, a man like him didn't just happen to be anywhere.

He nodded toward her bar. "Aren't you going to offer me a drink? Scotch, if you have it."

Monica went to the bar and fixed them both a drink. When she turned around, he was standing right behind her. She handed him the glass and invited him to sit on the sofa. As she watched him walk there, she had the unmistakable feeling this wasn't the first drink he'd had tonight.

"So, Monica," he said as they sat down. "Have you found out when you'll be able to come to work for me?"

"My boss hasn't been available for the past few days," she lied. "I'll have to get back to you."

"Andi Shaunessy is an interesting person," Jernigan said.

She didn't miss the emphasis he put on the word *interesting*.

"Yes. She is." But at least Andi didn't come to her house half drunk at eight o'clock at night. Monica picked up her drink, growing more annoyed by the second that he'd shown up here out of the blue.

Then she felt his hand on her knee.

She froze, her drink halfway to her lips. There it was. Proof positive of just what this man wanted from her, as if she had needed any proof at all.

She brought the drink the rest of the way to her lips, took a sip, then realized her hand was shaking and lowered it again.

It would be so easy to give him what he wanted because men could be so basic. A little hot sex opened up wallets and job opportunities and confidences of all kinds, and wasn't that what she wanted?

There's a lot to be said for self-respect.

She'd have to take Susan's word for that because she'd never experienced much of it herself. She'd always told herself that it gave her power to be sleeping with the boss. That way she had him under her thumb and could control her own fate. Then Jerry had shown her just how little power she actually had.

Would this man be any different?

She glanced around her condo. Buying this place had meant so much to her. Only now she realized how false it had all been. Her ability to buy it hadn't been based on her performance on the job. It had been based on her performance *outside* the job.

She looked down at Jernigan's hand on her knee, and the truth struck her hard. Putting herself at the beck and call of a wealthy, oversexed man was the act of a cheap and desperate woman. She took a deep, silent breath. She'd been that woman once.

She wasn't anymore.

She picked up Jernigan's hand, and placed it on the sofa, feeling as if she were jumping out of a ten-story window and praying there was a net.

He looked at her with surprise. "What are you doing?"

"Maybe I should ask you the same question."

"Now, Monica. You're hardly a neophyte. I was sure you understood the nature of the position you were being offered."

"Yes. I understood it very well."

"Then what seems to be the problem?"

"I've changed my mind, Mr. Jernigan. I don't believe I'm interested in the job after all."

He leaned away slightly, assessing this latest turn of events. "You must know that there are a lot of women who would jump at the position. As well as all the duties that come along with it."

"I'm quite sure there are. So I imagine one of them will be delighted to have the opportunity."

"Why are you reneging on me, Monica? Are you holding out for more money?"

"The money doesn't interest me."

"Why did you go to work for Andi Shaunessy? Were your job prospects that limited?"

"That's none of your business."

"I'll take that as a yes."

She set her glass on the table. "Actually, you're right.

Oddly enough, I discovered that job prospects for women my age aren't as plentiful as they are for younger women."

"So why are you turning this one down?"

"Why are you offering the job to me when you could have a woman half my age?"

"Because I like you, of course."

"And evidently you liked the stories Jerry told you about my job performance when I was working for him."

"Now, Monica," he said with a sly smile. "Do you actually think we discuss such things?"

"What I think," Monica said, "is that you get together at the club, have a couple of shots of hundred-year-old Scotch and swap sex stories every chance you get."

He met her gaze evenly. "And if not for women like you, we wouldn't have a thing to talk about."

With the sting of that comment ringing in her ears, she stood up. "Well, this is one woman you're never going to be able to talk about again. Good night, Mr. Jernigan."

A touch of anger flashed across his face. Clearly he was used to being the one who did the dismissing, not the other way around.

He stood up slowly and walked to the door. She opened it, and he stepped across the threshold onto the porch. Then slowly he turned back to look at her.

"There's only one thing worse than a man who hires

a woman for sex," he said. "And that's the woman who takes him up on it."

"I believe I turned down your job offer."

"For now, you have."

"What do you mean?"

"Women like you know how to operate only one way. A few more weeks at that low-end job at the hospital and you'll change your mind. And you'd better hope by then that I haven't already hired that younger woman. A taste of one of those, and I might not be so willing to go back to a woman old enough to be her mother."

Bastard.

Monica gripped the doorknob until her fingers turned white. He could have put his ego on hold, kept things civil and walked out of here without any mud-slinging. He'd chosen not to.

Bad move.

"You're lucky I'm fresh out of flowerpots, Jernigan, or I might be inspired to put one right through the windshield of that Jag of yours."

"And once again, you'd be facing assault charges."

"The satisfaction would be worth it."

"A whore *and* a jailbird. See how employable you'd be then."

"You know," Monica said, "I think I know why you offered me the job."

"Why?"

"Because you couldn't find a younger woman interested in sleeping with her *grandfather!*"

She slammed the door, only to yank it back open. "And just for the record…" She dropped her gaze to his crotch, then brought it slowly back up. "Men who drive Hummers aren't the only ones compensating for something."

She slammed the door again. After a moment, she heard a car door shut and an engine start. She looked out the peephole and watched him leave the parking lot, his taillights disappearing into the night.

She turned and leaned against the door, drawing in a deep, calming breath. She couldn't believe it. She'd actually done it. She'd just told one of the most powerful and wealthy men in town to shove his job offer. Not only that, she'd insulted his age and his manhood. Those things alone were enough to make him blackball her with every mover and shaker in Dallas.

Monica sat down on the sofa, picked up her drink and downed it, waiting to feel regret about that, but it never came. Strangely, the only thought that occurred to her was *Andi and Susan would be proud of you.*

Yes, Andi was dictatorial. Demanding. Overbearing. And nobody would ever mistake her for a warm and fuzzy human being. But she'd given Monica something no other boss ever had before: a good, hard kick in the pants. Then Susan had followed up with a one-two punch that had knocked so much sense into her that eventually she couldn't help but do the right thing. Both of them believed she was selling herself short and had given her something to live up to, and Monica had a feeling she was going to be thanking them for that for the rest of her life.

Tonya woke at seven the next morning, feeling as if she'd barely slept at all. But even though she felt like hell, still she rose and pulled herself together, arriving at the hospital at eight-thirty. She knew it was probably too early and Dale wasn't even awake yet, but she wanted to be there as soon as he got up.

She went down the hall to his room, slowing as she approached it, intending to peek inside first and not just barge in. As she approached the room, though, she heard voices. She stopped at the door and listened. One of them was Dale's. The other sounded like a woman's.

Tonya stopped and peered around the corner. A woman stood at Dale's bedside. She was young. Blond. Beautiful. Tonya watched them, straining to hear what they were saying, but she couldn't make out the words.

Then, to Tonya's surprise, the woman sat down on the edge of his bed. She put her palm against Dale's cheek, then leaned in and kissed the opposite one. When she backed away, he was smiling at her.

Tonya wanted to die.

This couldn't be happening. Suddenly her head was swimming with anger and humiliation. Who was the woman? Somebody Dale had been seeing since she'd moved out? Suddenly Tonya had the most terrible thought. Maybe Dale had been so slow about wanting to get back together because he had to make up his mind about another woman.

Tonya backed away from the door and walked halfway down the hall, so shook up she was trembling. A few minutes later, the woman came out of Dale's room. Tonya stood by the wall as she passed by, all the while trying to think of any reason why a woman she didn't recognize would be kissing her husband right there in his hospital room. And she couldn't come up with a single one.

Her face grew hot, her nerves poised to act. She had to know who the woman was.

Tonya started down the hall, sidestepping a nurse pushing a man in a wheelchair, then an elderly woman in a pink bathrobe. Ahead of her, the woman turned left at the nurse's station and walked toward the elevator. Tonya decided she'd follow her to the parking lot, where she could write down her license number. Maybe from that she could find out the woman's name. What she would do then, she didn't have a clue.

She managed to get to the elevator before the doors opened. Standing quietly beside the woman, her heart racing, Tonya pictured how she'd kissed Dale and how he'd smiled at her, and her stomach churned with jealousy.

She couldn't stand this. She just couldn't. What was she going to do if she lost this woman in the parking lot? If she never had the peace of mind of knowing that whoever she was, she meant nothing to Dale? How was she ever going to know the truth?

Then all at once, something Dale said last night flashed through her mind.

It's faith, honey. And that's it.

Tonya froze, playing those words over in her head. Several seconds passed; it was as if something dark in her mind fell away and light came streaming in. And that was when she realized that she finally understood.

No matter what the truth was about this woman's identity, about why she was at the hospital, there was a truth that was bigger than either of those things. Tonya didn't have to know who this woman was, because she knew who Dale was. He didn't have to prove anything to her, now or in the future. He already had, just by being the kind of man he was. The kind of man she should have had faith in. Why hadn't she been able to see that?

The elevator dinged and the doors opened. The woman got on, punched a button for her floor and waited, watching Tonya. When the elevator doors started to close, she reached out a hand to stop them.

"Are you coming?" she asked.

Tonya gave her a little smile. "No. Go ahead."

The woman moved her hand, and the elevator

doors closed. Tonya stood there a long time, waiting for that feeling that she was a fool because she hadn't gotten to the bottom of this.

It never came.

She headed back down the hall to Dale's room. When she went inside, she saw him reading the sports page. She sat down in the chair next to him, not surprised in the least to see lipstick on his cheek.

"They're letting me go around two," he said.

"Good. I'll take you home."

He nodded, then flipped on the TV and they watched some talk show. Tonya didn't hear a word of it. She still felt the trouble between them, like an elephant in the room they couldn't get around.

After about half an hour, Dale got up to go to the bathroom. He was in there for a few minutes, and when he came back out, he held a tissue with a pale smear of red, and the lipstick was no longer on his face. He just stood there staring at her.

"Did you see this?"

She put her magazine aside. "The lipstick? Yes."

Dale stared at her with surprise. "You've been looking at lipstick on my face for half an hour, and you didn't say anything?"

"That's right."

"Do you know where it came from?"

"Yes."

He looked at her skeptically. "Where?"

"From the blond woman who was here earlier. I saw her kiss you."

His eyes widened with disbelief. "And you didn't say anything about it?"

"That's right."

He came over and sat down on the bed, looking at her as if he was waiting for her to speak. Tonya just stared back at him.

"Aren't you going to ask me who the woman was?" Dale said.

"Nope."

"Do you want to know?"

"Nope."

Dale looked confused. "I'm sorry, but that's a little hard for me to believe."

"I know. You're expecting flying bedpans. And that's okay. I don't blame you for that, because God knows you've had to duck a few things in the past."

"Am I getting a pass because I'm in the hospital?"

"Nope."

"Okay, I don't get this. I've been known to get in hot water because I looked at another woman across the room. Now you see a woman kissing me, and nothing. You say you don't even know who she was. What makes you think I'm not cheating on you this time?"

Tears sprang to Tonya's eyes because now that she had the whole picture, she hated that she'd wasted so much time being so blind. Why had it taken her so long to know the heart of the man she'd married and to give him her heart without hesitation, knowing he'd always protect it?

"It's faith, honey," she said. "And that's it."

Dale stared at her a long time, so long that she wondered whether he believed her or not. But at least she knew he wanted to believe. Dale was like that. Always wanting to believe the best about people.

"Is it really that simple for you?" he asked.

"No. It's not simple at all. It's the hardest thing ever. But I finally figured something out."

"What's that?"

"That it's my problem and not yours, and it's up to me to work it out in my own head. From now on, that's what I'm going to do."

Maybe he believed her. Maybe he didn't. But all she could do was keep telling him until he finally accepted it.

"Where does it come from?" Dale asked. "All the jealousy?"

"It's not really that. Not deep down."

"Then what is it?"

She wasn't completely sure. It had been coming to her in bits and pieces over the last few weeks, but still she felt so confused that she was afraid if she tried to tell him about it, she'd only make things worse.

But maybe things couldn't get any worse.

"I watched my father cheat," she said. "Then two stepfathers did the same thing. Then my ex-husband."

"I know you've been hurt in the past, Tonya, but I'm not those men."

"I know. But after I'd been through all that, you came along, and we got married…" She paused, feeling her throat tighten up. "And I was *so* scared."

"Scared? Of what?"

"Losing you."

"Losing me? Why would you think that?"

"You're something special, Dale. I could tell even in the beginning because of how much you'd loved Alison and how many friends you had and the family you came from. That's where the scary part came in. I just found it so hard to believe that you could possibly love somebody like me."

Her throat tightened up again. She swallowed hard, but her voice was a harsh whisper. "Even the day we got married, I remember thinking, please God, don't let him cheat. Just let him love me and only me."

A look of understanding passed over his face. "And then you thought I had cheated."

"What I did wasn't smart. It wasn't even particularly sane. Like I said, it had nothing to do with you and everything to do with what was in my own head." Her eyes filled with tears. "Do you see what I mean? Take a good, hard look at who you married. To this day, I still can't figure out why you did it."

His face slowly changed. His eyes softened. When he spoke, his voice wasn't harsh or distant. It was Dale's again.

"Because you were exactly who I needed."

Tonya blinked with surprise. "What do you mean?"

"I was such a mess after Alison died. Other women walked on eggshells around me, and no wonder. The poor widower, they were thinking, with all that baggage. But not you. You told me you knew how much I'd loved her, but she was the one who had died and not me, and I had a life I had to get back to."

"That's kinda the way I deal with everything," she said with a sigh. "Sometimes that's good, and sometimes it isn't."

For the first time in weeks, a soft smile lit his face. "That time," he said, "it was good."

It was good. Those words sounded so beautiful coming out of his mouth. And that smile. God, how she'd missed it.

"That was why I fell in love with you," he said. "Because you made me feel so alive when I'd been dead inside for so long. I needed that."

Hope swelled inside Tonya, but she could hardly find her voice to ask the question.

"Do you still?"

Several seconds passed, and her heart was beating like crazy. But Dale was still smiling.

He held out his hand.

Swallowing hard, she put her hand in his, and he pulled her over to sit next to him on the bed. When he put his arm around her and turned to kiss her hair, tears started down her cheeks.

"It's only been you, Tonya. From the day we got married. Only you."

And then she really did cry. She'd screwed everything up so much, yet here he was holding her and hugging her, and because of that the crying felt good. It seemed to release every bit of the tension she'd felt all these weeks. She sat there crying until there weren't any tears left and he was just holding her quietly in his arms.

"She was one of the women I pulled out of that burning apartment building," Dale said. "She heard I was in the hospital and came by to thank me."

Tonya didn't feel so much as a tremor of relief. And that was because she knew the truth before Dale told her the truth. He'd just filled in the details.

"She got a little carried away," Dale said. "It was actually kind of embarrassing."

"Of course she got carried away. That lifesaving thing is bigger than you want to admit." Tonya sniffed and wiped her eyes. "For someone who's not prone to crying, I sure have done a lot of it recently."

Dale rubbed his hand up and down her arm. "I know where you came from," he said softly. "I know it's hard to trust. But just keep on doing it, and I swear to God I'll never give you a reason to regret it."

And there he was, making promises to her when she was the one who'd caused all these problems in the first place. She also realized he wasn't just talking about now, but the future.

She looked up at him. "Dale?"

"Yeah?"

"Do you think we're going to be okay again?"

He smiled. "I think there's a good chance of that."

In the dark of night sometimes, Tonya knew she'd probably still feel a little scared, still have those little twinges when another woman looked at Dale. Maybe a lot of them. But there was no way she was going to let any of her dumb insecurities mess up the best thing that had ever happened to her. After all, how many women could say they were married to a man who they knew in their heart would love them and be faithful to them for the rest of their lives?

CHAPTER 18

Later that morning, when Monica called Susan and asked her if she wanted to have lunch with her in the hospital cafeteria, Susan thought it might be a trap. After the fight they'd had last night over that job at Wyatt Industries, she wondered if Monica was planning to lure her into the cafeteria, then go off on her in a way that would make what Susan had done to Dennis look tame.

But when Susan got there, Monica greeted her with a smile, told her she'd decided to stay at the hospital and gave her a great big hug. They grabbed lunch, and Monica told Susan the story of how Jernigan had shown up for a booty call last night and she'd booted him right out the door.

Susan couldn't believe it. After last night, she would have sworn Monica was going to take that job at Wyatt Industries and kiss her job here goodbye, and she was absolutely thrilled that she hadn't.

Then they saw Tonya, who'd come downstairs to get a bite of lunch. She sat with them, and when Susan saw she was smiling, too, she ventured the question.

"So how are things going with you and Dale?"

Tonya's smile grew even wider. "Good. They're good."

"So…?"

"So when he goes home today, I'm going home with him."

"Oh, Tonya! That's wonderful!"

"You finally patched things up?" Monica said.

Tonya told them the story of what had happened between them, and it was all Susan could do not to cry. Then Monica told Tonya that she'd decided to forego the career path that involved sleeping with the boss in favor of continuing to work for Andi.

Tonya turned to Susan. "How are you and Paul?"

"Things are really good," Susan said, then paused, still feeling a little confused. "I think they are, anyway. I mean, things are fine with Paul and me. It's Lani who's kind of weird."

"What do you mean?"

She told them the story of how she and Paul had run into Lani the night they went to the movie.

"Oh, boy," Tonya said. "Couldn't you have just pretended Paul was a friend or something?"

"Hard to do when Lani saw him kiss me."

"Uh-oh," Monica said. "So what happened?"

"She threw a fit and stomped out of the theater. But when Don brought her home the next day, she told me she didn't care if I dated Paul. She's being very nice about it."

"Isn't that what you want?"

"*Too* nice," Susan said pointedly. "Know what I mean?"

"Hmm," Monica said. "When I was in high school, I was once sickeningly sweet to my mother for a week before I asked her if I could take a trip to Austin with my boyfriend."

"That's exactly the kind of thing I'm afraid of."

"Have you asked Lani why she changed her mind?" Tonya asked.

"I didn't press her on that. I don't want to rock the boat."

"Maybe she's just being sweet," Monica said. "Kids do eventually grow up, you know."

"God, I hope so. Because this thing with Paul…" She couldn't help the ridiculous smile that came over her face. "He's the best thing that's happened to me in a very long time."

The basketball game the next day turned out to be every bit the enjoyable experience Susan had anticipated. She got there a little early and decided to sit lower on the bleachers than she usually did, and a few minutes later Don and Marla showed up. She didn't even get a chance to tell them she had a friend coming when she saw Paul at the door of the gym. She raised her hand and waved to him, and when he walked over, sat down and gave Susan a kiss, she thought Don's eyes were going to pop out of his head.

She introduced Paul to both of them, and everyone made nice. Don, however, was clearly freaked out. Susan knew it had nothing to do with jealousy. He just didn't like the people in his realm changing any more than his daughter liked it, and his ex-wife dating another man screwed up the status quo something awful. But since the status quo of late had really sucked, screwing it up could only be a good thing.

The best thing of all was Lani's attitude. She came up during the pregame warm-up and said hello to everyone, including Paul, and there wasn't so much as an ounce of resentment in her expression, her posture or her voice.

Susan had decided to go with the pod people theory. She'd gotten a whole new replacement child. Now, if only that replacement child had a better memory than the original, got straight As and hated talking on the telephone, Susan would have definitely gotten the better end of the deal.

Another thing that was funny was how little it irritated Susan to be in that smelly, noisy gym when she was with Paul. It was as if she couldn't even hear that godawful buzzer or the squeak of athletic shoes on the floor. He turned out to be a pretty big basketball fan, and it looked to Susan as if he was actually having a good time. When he slipped his hand over hers and held it, she remembered what it felt like to fall in love and wished she hadn't waited all this time to rediscover the feeling.

After the game, Lani jogged over and told them she was starving. Evidently she'd skipped dinner with the team to work on her history paper in the computer lab, and the snacks this time were something gross with dates in them.

Linda Markham had struck again.

Marla told Lani there was something she wanted to talk to her about anyway, so she and Don offered to take her by McDonald's for a burger and then bring her home, which was fine by Susan.

While Don and Marla waited in the gym for Lani to change shoes and grab her backpack, Paul walked Susan to her car. When she shivered in the cold, Paul opened his coat. She reached inside, wrapped her arms around him, and he closed the coat around her. It felt heavenly.

"So what do you think?" Paul said. "Lani doesn't seem to have a problem with me being here."

"I still don't get it. Do you think she's actually coming around?"

"Looks that way. Did you hear her tell Don she liked your new haircut and ask him if he thought it was pretty?"

"Now, *that's* unbelievable."

"No, it's not. Your hair *is* pretty."

"But moms usually aren't pretty to their daughters. They're just…well, *moms*."

"Well, you may be a mom to her, but…"

Paul dipped his head to give her a good-night kiss. It started out short and sweet, only to become long and spicy, and Susan couldn't believe what a lucky woman she'd turned out to be.

They said goodbye, and Susan headed home. She got ready for bed, relishing the peace in the household once again. Somehow life had turned around. The sun was shining. Birds were singing. She felt as if she were living in a Disney movie, complete with cute little forest creatures and a nice, happy ending.

Putting on her robe, she went to the kitchen to make herself a cup of tea, then grabbed the novel she was reading. She had just settled onto the sofa to have a few quiet moments to herself, when she heard footsteps on the porch. The front door burst open and Lani appeared.

Susan sat up suddenly. "Lani?"

She blew right past Susan and went to her room, slamming the door behind her. When Susan turned back around, Don and Marla were coming into the house carrying McDonald's sacks.

Susan rose from the sofa. "What's going on?"

"I don't know," Don said. "She was perfectly fine until we sat down to eat and Marla started talking to her about being a bridesmaid at our wedding. Lani threw a fit. Marla was only being nice, and Lani treated her horribly. She said she didn't want to be in the wedding. She said she didn't even want to *come* to the wedding."

Frustration welled up inside Susan until she wanted to scream. She felt as if her whole life had moved two steps forward, one step back. Just when she thought she was out of the woods with Lani, she was stuck in the trees all over again. And if Lani still resented her father and Marla getting married, it meant she and Paul were in trouble, too.

It was just as she'd thought. All of Lani's "one big happy family" stuff was a crock. But what was really going on?

"She's being totally unreasonable about the wedding," Don said. "You have to talk to her."

"Excuse me?" Susan said. "*I* have to talk to her? Why?"

"I don't get why she's so upset. I thought girls liked weddings. Wearing those dresses and everything. I know she's only fourteen, but Marla will pick out something nice."

"It's not about the dress, Don," Susan said, rolling her eyes. "She doesn't want you to get married."

Don blinked. "She doesn't?"

"Ohh," Marla said, nodding with understanding. "Now everything's making sense."

"What's making sense?" Don said.

"I'm sorry, Susan," Marla said. "I had no idea. Lani hasn't said anything negative about it up to now, even the night we told her, so I assumed she was all right with it."

"She *is* all right with it!" Don said. "Why wouldn't she want us to get married? Marla's been nothing but nice to her!"

"Marla has nothing to do with it," Susan told him. "She'd resent any woman you were marrying."

"Well, you have to fix this! Talk to her!"

Translation: *You go in there. You stick your head in the grizzly bear's mouth. You be the bad guy for the umpteenth time.*

This time she wasn't going to do it.

Susan was finally beginning to realize that she wasn't responsible for the happiness of every person in her realm of influence, and she most certainly wasn't getting in the middle of this. Since it was Dad's actions that instigated the problem, Dad was going to fix it.

"It's your wedding," Susan said. "She's your daughter. *You* deal with it."

Don sighed. He glanced toward Lani's bedroom, and Susan could see his wheels turning. *How the hell do I get out of this?*

"It's probably best to let her settle down first, don't you think?"

"No," Susan said. "I don't think."

"She's really emotional right now. If I try to talk to her, things will get ugly."

"Then bring on ugly."

"It would only cause a scene."

"I'll make popcorn."

"Susan," he said sharply. "You're being unreasonable. You're better at talking to her than I am."

"Yeah, I'm a real pro at it. That's because I've had plenty of practice. Now it's your turn to step up to the plate."

"This is ridiculous. If we just let a little time pass, this will blow over all by itself. Come on, Marla," he said, standing up. "We need to go."

"Sit," Marla said.

Don blinked. And sat.

"Susan?" Marla said. "If you'll ask Lani to come out here, Don will have a talk with her." She turned and raised an eyebrow at Don. "Won't you?"

"Look, I really don't think—"

"*Won't you?*"

Don closed his eyes. "Yeah. I'd be thrilled to."

A minute later, Lani was sitting in a chair in the living room, looking as sulky as ever. And Don looked as oblivious as ever.

"So…your mother tells me you're not really happy about Marla and me getting married. Is that right?"

Lani spun around to Susan. "You *told* him that?"

"It wasn't as if I couldn't figure it out," Don said, even though he obviously hadn't. "As soon as Marla started talking about bridesmaid dresses, you flipped out."

"I'm not wearing some old-lady dress!"

"But Marla has good taste. I'm sure she'll pick out something—"

"Don," Marla said quietly. "It's not about the dress."

Don let out a breath. "Look, I know you don't like Marla. But pretty soon you're going to realize—"

Lani turned to Susan. "Mom! You told him that, *too?*"

Don bowed his head, clearly wishing he were anywhere else on the planet. Finally he looked up again.

"Your mother also told me it was your idea for her to bring Paul to your basketball game. And that you wanted me and Marla there, too, and it seemed as if you were happy about all of it. So what changed?"

Lani turned away, folding her arms.

"We're just trying to figure out what's going on."

She was silent.

"Lani, you need to tell me—"

"All right! I thought if Mom showed up there with that guy, you'd get jealous and maybe you'd want her back!"

Don sat back, stunned. "Is that why you told me you saw them kissing at the movie the other night?"

"Yes," Lani snapped.

Now Susan remembered Paul telling her about the remark Lani had made to Don about her hair being pretty and asking her father if he thought so, too. Now she knew why.

"What in the world made you think I'd get jealous

of your mother going out with another man?" Don asked.

"It worked for Kaylee when her parents were separated."

Don turned to Susan. "Kaylee's parents were separated?"

"Don? Will you stay on topic? Please?"

"Then you and Marla started talking about bridesmaid dresses," Lani went on, "and that's when I knew you didn't care. You didn't care if Mom was with another guy. It was Marla you wanted."

"That's right," Don said.

Lani's eyes teared up. "I just want things back the way they were."

"Come on, Lani," Don said. "Would you really want things the way they used to be when your mom and I were married? Would you really rather go back to a time when everyone was so unhappy?"

"It's just that everything is changing. You have Marla. And now Mom is seeing that guy. And she changed her hair and her clothes and everything."

Lani turned away, her frown deepening.

"Look," Don said, "I'm sorry you're having a problem with me and Marla getting married and with your mother seeing Paul. But you're not a little girl anymore. You're old enough to understand that things can never go back to the way they were and that we deserve to be happy, too."

"Even if I'm not?"

"You could be if you wanted to."

"I'll never be happy again."

"But—"

"*Never!*"

"Okay, that's it!" Don said sharply. "I don't want to hear another word!"

Lani recoiled, looking stunned, and Susan was equally surprised. What the hell was he doing?

"What you did tonight was wrong," Don said. "Dead wrong. You're trying to manipulate us, and I resent that. Your mother and I have moved past the divorce and are making new lives for ourselves. Unfortunately, you've decided you don't want to move on with us. You were horrible to Marla tonight, you were horrible to me and apparently you've been horrible to your mom for some time now. You want to be unhappy about the divorce, and you want everyone else to be unhappy, too. But if we refuse to be, where does that leave you?"

Lani's eyes grew even wider, and Susan braced herself for the explosion. She could already hear the stomping and the door slamming and picture the days of silent treatment she was going to have to endure when all this was over.

"Here's the deal, Lani," Don said. "You can be miserable at your own little pity party, or you can join our party and be happy. Which is it going to be?"

For at least thirty seconds, nobody said a word. Don continued to stare at Lani and she stared back, as if she couldn't believe her father had actually issued an ultimatum. Susan couldn't believe it. He just wasn't an ultimatum kind of guy. Avoidance. That was his thing. But now this?

Lani frowned. "I guess I have to join yours."

Don sat back. "Good choice."

Susan's mouth fell open. That actually worked? Then just as quickly, she clamped it shut again. No sense acting surprised. Who knew when she'd need Attack Dad again in the future?

"I know you don't like everything changing," Don said. "But for us, you're changing, too."

"I'm not changing."

"Of course you are. You're growing up. That's hard on parents sometimes."

"You guys are the ones who are different, not me."

"Lani, if you weren't different, you'd still be listening to nursery rhymes instead of that god-awful crap that—"

Marla nudged his thigh. He shot her a look of irritation. She raised an eyebrow. He sighed and turned back to Lani.

"Instead of those *wonderful* young musicians you listen to now," he said, practically choking on the words. "One of these days, you're going to start dating. Would you want us to tell you that you couldn't do that just because we don't like it when things change?"

"No. I guess not. But—"

"And would you want us to tell you we hate any boys you date?"

"No, but—"

"I'm not really interested in any 'buts,' Lani. It all boils down to the fact that your mom and I are a whole lot happier, and we want you to be, too. Now, are you at least going to try?"

Lani looked back and forth between her mother and father with an expression that said happiness might still be a long time coming.

Finally she rolled her eyes. "Fine. I'll try."

Susan didn't know exactly what Lani's trying was going to consist of, and the *Leave It to Beaver* moment she'd hoped for evidently wasn't going to materialize, but after what they'd been through lately grudging acceptance was a definite step up.

"I'm still starving," Lani muttered.

"Okay," Susan said. "Everybody to the kitchen, and I'll heat up the food."

"The fries will be gross by now," Lani said.

"I'll grab a bag of chips."

"Sounds good to me," Don said.

"Me, too," Marla said.

"Lani?" Susan said. "Did I see Mrs. Markham passing out notes to the girls after the game?"

"Yeah."

Great. Susan couldn't even imagine what Linda had waiting for her this time.

"Would you mind bringing it to me?"

Lani rose from her chair and disappeared into her bedroom, and the three of them let out a collective sigh.

"I used to know what to say to her," Don said. "It was easy. Now it's not so easy."

"Yeah," Susan said. "Once they outgrow the 'Do you want a Happy Meal?' phase, things get rough."

Don closed his eyes. "Don't make me do that very often."

"Like once every fourteen years?"

"Yeah. With luck, she'll be over all this by age twenty-eight."

"Sorry. You're not off the hook. You're dealing with her problems from now on, too."

Don looked a little sick at the thought of that. He glanced at Marla, who nodded in agreement with Susan. He dropped his head to the back of the sofa with a sigh.

"And another thing," Susan said. "The next time you're going out of town like you did to San Francisco and can't see Lani, I need more notice. Three days isn't good enough."

Marla turned to Don with a look of disbelief. "You didn't tell her until three days before we left?"

"I forgot."

Susan crossed her arms. "You said you were just being spontaneous."

"Spontaneous?" Marla said. "We'd been planning that trip for a month." She whacked Don's arm with the back of her hand. "Don't do that to Susan."

"Hey, I said I forgot!"

"Well, don't forget again. That's inconsiderate."

When Don looked properly chastised, Susan decided she liked Marla more with each passing moment. It occurred to her that if, just once in sixteen years of marriage, she'd smacked Don and told him to stop being inconsiderate, things between them might have turned out differently.

They went to the kitchen. Lani came into the room and handed Susan the note. Yep. Linda was at it again.

"I'm supposed to bring cheese chewies?"

"Jennifer's mom made those once. They're disgusting."

"Wait a minute. Didn't I just send granola bars? How can it be my turn again next week?"

"Two snacks per game, two or three games a week, ten kids on the team. It cycles around pretty quick. Plus, Sarah's mother's out of town."

Susan was surprised Linda didn't make the poor woman FedEx something from wherever she happened to be.

"Do you and your friends like any of that stuff Linda Markham has all the mothers make?"

"Some of it's okay," Lani said, sitting down at the kitchen table. "But there was that time she brought goose liver pâté to the band picnic."

"Goose liver pâté?" Marla said, her face crinkled with disgust. "For junior high kids?"

"The basketball snacks are usually gross. Wheat germ crispies. Cinnamon rice cakes. Fake cocoa brownies with raisins in them."

"Yuk," Marla said.

"Yuk is right," Don agreed.

"Eat your Big Mac," Susan told Lani. "That'll help counteract all the healthy stuff."

Susan sat down and munched on a few chips, and as she looked around the table a strange sense of satisfaction settled over her. Lani suddenly felt less like that grizzly bear and more like an irritated little cub. Susan didn't delude herself into thinking that Don had suddenly become Superdad, but it was nice to know that Lani's upbringing wasn't all on her shoulders anymore. After all, she had Marla in her corner. In spite of that sweet little face, she wasn't above doing what it took to keep Don in line. To have her ex-husband's fiancée as an ally during "family wars" was something Susan had never expected. Suddenly Marla had been elevated from the woman she wished she could hate to the woman she liked very much.

Then she thought about Paul.

For the first time in so long, she felt like a singular

woman in her own right, unconnected by invisible chains to an ex-husband or a demanding daughter, and Paul was a big reason why. He'd told her she deserved to be happy, too, and it looked as if it was finally going to happen.

CHAPTER 19

At the basketball game on Friday night, Lani managed to greet all of them with a minimum of bad attitude, although she undoubtedly still felt as if they were paired up all wrong. Her team won the game by only two points, but that was because of a three-point shot Lani made in the last twenty seconds, and Susan thought Don was going to wet his pants with excitement over that.

At the final buzzer, Susan turned to Paul. "Will you excuse me for a minute? I have to take snacks to the girls' locker room. I'll be right back."

He nodded and gave her a quick kiss. She climbed down off the bleachers and went to the locker room. Linda was there already, setting out napkins and paper plates. Why, Susan didn't know. The girls usually just grabbed food off the table, stuffed it into their mouths and wiped their hands on their shorts.

Barbara Huffman was there, too, with a Tupperware container full of soy nut delights, cookielike creations that looked, and tasted, like dog biscuits. A couple of other mothers were hanging around chatting, waiting for their daughters.

"Hello, Susan," Linda said. "I hope you didn't have trouble finding the ingredients for the cheese chewies."

"Uh, yeah, Linda...about that..."

Susan walked over to the table, turned the bag she held upside down, and three dozen fun-size Snickers bars tumbled onto the table. The other mothers' eyes flew open wide. Barbara Huffman held her container of soy nut delights so tightly her fingers whitened.

Linda stared down at the candy with horror. "What do you think you're *doing?*"

"Bringing snacks."

"You were supposed to bring cheese chewies! The girls can't eat these!"

"Oh, I'm betting they can. I'm betting they do. And I'm betting they do it *very* quickly."

"Not if I have anything to say about it!"

Linda reached toward the table, and she had just closed her fist around a pair of the Snickers bars when Susan grabbed her wrist. Linda spun her head around, her eyes wide with surprise.

"Listen up, Linda," Susan said. "From now on, if you ask me for trifle, you're getting Twinkies. If you ask for walnut date cookies, you're getting Fig Newtons. If you ask for brioche, you're getting a loaf of Wonder Bread. That's just the way it's going to be."

The other women stood by, frozen in disbelief.

"The bottom line is that you may have time for this nonsense, but I don't. Now," she said, slowly releasing Linda's wrist, "step *away* from the Snickers."

Linda backed away, stunned, then turned to the other mothers. "Are you going to let your girls eat nothing but sugar and fat and preservatives?"

Barbara Huffman stared at her for a moment, then walked across the room and upended her container of soy nut delights into the trash can. Linda gasped and sputtered, her hand at her throat, trying to dislodge the scream of horror that was trapped there.

The girls came into the locker room, saw the candy bars on the table and descended on them like a swarm of locusts wiping out a wheat crop. Susan didn't think she'd ever seen anyone look quite as pissed as Linda did at that moment.

"Melissa!" she said to her daughter, who had one of the Snickers halfway to her mouth. "Put that down!"

But Melissa had been eating soy nut delights and cheese chewies all this time, too, and somehow that Snickers ended up *in* her mouth.

"Oops," she said. "Sorry, Mom."

Oops, indeed.

Linda grabbed her by the arm and hustled her out of the locker room, and the other mothers turned to Susan with smiles of delighted disbelief. But the biggest smile of all came from Lani, who looked at her as if she'd braved enemy fire to drop supplies to war-ravaged troops.

Susan smiled back. *Ding dong, the witch is dead.*

On Monday night, Susan was surprised to feel a little wistful that their last class was nearly over but certainly not because she'd miss Danforth. He rambled on most of the evening about how to use compromise in place of conflict, expressing his thoughts in his usual overblown manner. Then he had them do some role-playing to practice those techniques. After that, he suggested that each of them keep a journal for several months to record any instances of anger and how they dealt with it. Susan figured Tonya and Monica were about as eager to do that as she was.

It just didn't feel the least bit necessary.

Tonya was surprisingly mellow all evening. She didn't make any smart remarks or ask Danforth to define a single word even though there were several good opportunities to do so. As he lectured, she just sat there with her arms folded and a look on her face that told Susan her mind was elsewhere, probably somewhere in the vicinity of her husband.

Near the end of the class, Danforth warned them he was wrapping up and asked them if they had any questions. Tonya raised her hand.

"Yes, Ms. Rutherford?"

"We've been talking for weeks now about different

methods we should use to deal with our anger. How do you manage yours when it gets out of hand?"

He gave her a condescending little smirk. "My anger doesn't get out of hand. Reactionary behavior is the hallmark of small-minded people with no self-control. I trust I've taught you ladies how to put all that behind you."

Susan shared a furtive "you gotta be kidding" look with Tonya and Monica, but they all nodded dutifully, visions of martinis dancing in their heads.

"Now, I don't want you going away feeling as if you're not empowered just because you needed professional help," Danforth said. "When one has a significant anger problem, one can't expect to solve it on one's own."

Susan smiled to herself, thinking about how they'd solved a lot of problems in the past eight weeks, but anger had been the least of them. She'd come to the conclusion that sometimes it was useful to control your anger, but sometimes it was better to fix those issues in your life that were making you crazy so they would never be issues again. Anger management classes hadn't helped much with that, but her unlikely friendship with two other women at their own crossroads certainly had.

At nine o'clock, Danforth did as he'd done every Monday night for the past seven weeks. He closed his notebook, lifted that beak of a nose a few inches in the air and said, "Class dismissed."

As he launched into his usual post-class note taking and paper shuffling, they all rose from their chairs and started for the door. Tonya, though, stopped and turned back. She looked at Danforth for a moment, then walked over to him.

He never looked up from his papers. "Yes, Ms. Rutherford?"

"I just wanted you to know something."

"Yes?"

"You pointed out that maybe my husband wasn't cheating and that maybe I should give him the benefit of the doubt. And you know what? It turned out you were right." She gave him a sincere smile. "Thank you."

Susan was astonished. Was Tonya actually swallowing her dislike of this man long enough to tell him he was right about something? And to *thank* him? Ahh. Susan was such a sap for warm, heartfelt moments. That Disney thing again.

"Of course I was right, Ms. Rutherford. I'm an expert on human behavior. I'm pleased to see that you're finally accepting your predisposition toward insecurity and overreaction. I trust you'll be able to judge potentially negative situations with more objectivity in the future?"

Tonya looked stunned for a moment. Her smile melted away, and her mouth became a grim line of irritation. When her eyes narrowed into little slits,

Susan decided that waiting for the explosion wasn't a good thing. She grabbed Tonya by the arm and pulled her to the door with Monica following close behind.

"Goodbye, Dr. Danforth," Susan called out as they left the room. "Thanks again."

Once they were in the hall, Tonya shook Susan's hand loose and spun around. "Did you hear what that little creep said to me?"

"Uh-huh. And the last thing you want is to be sentenced to eight more weeks of this. Now, let's go have a martini and forget all about it."

Monica and Susan each took an arm and led Tonya to the elevator, with her muttering the whole way there. They went down the elevator to the parking garage, and Monica and Susan headed for their cars.

Tonya headed for Danforth's Chevy Caprice.

Monica stopped. "Tonya?" she said, her voice sliding up in warning. "What are you doing?"

Tonya reached into her purse and pulled out her keys, walked around the car and knelt by the right rear tire. Susan watched with amazement as she stuck the key into the valve and air hissed out.

"Tonya! What are you doing?"

"So he's above getting angry, is he? Let's see if he practices what he preaches."

"That's vandalism!"

"Comes naturally. I was a juvenile delinquent."

"Are you sure that's his car?"

"Yeah. I got here the same time he did last week. Now, you two get behind Susan's car. I'll be there in a minute."

Susan and Monica crouched down behind Susan's car, then rose a little and peered through the windows, watching as Tonya rendered Danforth's tire as flat as roadkill. There were still a few dozen cars in the garage, and Susan hoped nobody came out before Tonya finished the job.

Then Susan heard a faint *ding*. "Tonya! The elevator! He's coming!"

Tonya ran over and crouched behind the car with them. After a few seconds, the door opened and Danforth strolled up to his car, his briefcase clutched in one hand. He started to move around to the driver's door, only to stop short and stare down at the right rear tire. He stood there a long time as if assessing the situation.

"Look at that," Susan whispered. "He really is Mr. Calm, Cool and Collected."

Then all at once his body tensed. His face got crinkled and crabby. He gave the tire a hard kick, and his sharp voice echoed off the walls of the parking garage.

"Shit, shit, *shit!*"

He drew back, shouted another obscenity and kicked the tire again. Then he yanked his cell phone out of his briefcase and made a snotty phone call to his auto club.

The women stared at each other with amazement

before exploding in peals of muffled laughter. They shushed each other, then laughed some more.

"An hour?" Danforth said. "What do you mean, an *hour?*"

After a few more minutes of fuming at the person on the other end, he hung up the phone, stuffed it into his briefcase and marched back into the building. The moment the door closed behind him, the women came to their feet, only to double over with laughter.

"I've got an idea," Tonya said. "Why don't we really mess with his mind and change the tire?"

Their laughter surged, the women laughed again, the crazy, rollicking kind that made them run out of breath and tears come to their eyes. Before long, Susan's whole body was tingling with the joy of it and she couldn't remember the last time in her life when that had happened.

"Well, ladies," Susan said. "I think we've learned something here today, haven't we?"

"Yeah," Tonya said. "Danforth is a small-minded person with no self-control."

And then they were laughing all over again.

Soon they collected themselves, Susan's grin fading into a soft smile. "Actually, it's kinda nice to know he's human after all."

"Maybe, but I still can't stand him," Tonya said.

"No," Monica said. "I think what you mean to say

is, 'His personality is indicative of the type of individual I find particularly odious.'"

Tonya turned to Susan. "She's starting to enjoy being Danforth more than he does."

"Which tells me it's time for a drink," Susan said, pulling her keys out of her purse. "Shall we go?"

Later, as they sat on bar stools at the Fireside Grill, Susan looked around the table and saw nothing but good things. Tonya was rebuilding her relationship with Dale. Monica was improving hers with Andi. Susan was creating a new one with Paul. And before the evening was over, they'd decided to make Monday nights girls' night out every week, because none of them wanted to let go of the friendships they'd created with one another.

Susan couldn't believe it. For the first time in her life, she finally had it all: a good family situation, good friends, good gin and a good relationship that was full of possibilities for the future. It didn't get any better than that.

Stability is highly overrated....

Dana Logan's world had always revolved around her children. Now they're all grown up and don't seem to need anything she's able to give them. Struggling to find her new identity, Dana realizes that it's about time for her to get "off her rocker" and begin a new life!

Off Her Rocker

by Jennifer Archer

HN53

Available August 2006
TheNextNovel.com

HARLEQUIN®
Next™

Life on Long Island can be murder!

Teddi Bayer's life hasn't been what you'd call easy lately. Last year she'd never seen a dead person up close, but this year she discovered one. And it's her first paying client.... But Teddi is about to learn that when life throws you a curveball, there's no better time to take control of your own destiny.

What Goes with Blood Red, Anyway?

by Stevi Mittman

HARLEQUIN®
Next™

It's the time for courage, to love and be loved.

Francesca Bond has been surviving her life
much more than she has been living it.
Late one summer's night, things take a
dramatic turn and she finds herself running
from her bleak existence and into a
welcoming new world. Francesca soon
awakens to her heart's desire and
discovers the courage to live.

Awakening

by Kate Austin

Available July 2006
TheNextNovel.com

HN52

When life gets shaky... you've just gotta dance!

Learning to Hula
by Lisa Childs

Life.
It could happen to her!

Never Happened just about sums up
Alexis Jackson's life. Independent and
successful, Alexis has concentrated on
building her own business, leaving no
time for love. Now at forty, Alexis
discovers that she still has a few things
to learn about life—that the life unlived
is the one that "Never happened"
and it's her time to make a change....

Never Happened
by Debra Webb

Available July 2006
TheNextNovel.com

HN49

HARLEQUIN®
Next™

Just let it shine, it's payback time!

When a surprise inheritance brings
an unlikely pair together, the fortune
in sparkling jewelery could give
each woman what she desires most.
But the real treasure is the friendship
that forms when they discover that
all that glitters isn't gold.

Sparkle

by
Jennifer Greene

Available July 2006
TheNextNovel.com

HN50

HARLEQUIN
Ne̶xt

REQUEST YOUR FREE BOOKS!

2 FREE NOVELS TO INTRODUCE YOU TO OUR BRAND-NEW LINE!

There's the life you planned. And there's what comes next.